"Don't scream or—"

Jason sprawled on top of Kimberly on the queen-size bed, enjoying the feel of warm female curves pressed against him as she struggled.

"Or what?" she demanded. "You'll clamp your hand over my mouth again?"

He grinned and nestled between her thighs. "If you don't like my hand, maybe I could kiss you instead."

"Oh, please." She twisted her strong yet sensual body. Her hips were narrow, her waist slender and her lovely breasts revealed tight nipples that suggested she wasn't objecting that much. In fact, she seemed very aroused. As was he.

They were in a hotel room, on a bed. He could have her undressed in five seconds and then he could nibble a sleek path down her neck. Feast on those pert nipples. Savor that lush... No, he shouldn't.

"Stop thrashing around." Jason sighed. "We need to talk."

She panted and began to move beneath him again. "Let me go. There's nothing to talk about."

"If you don't want to talk, can I assume all your thrashing around is simply foreplay?"

Dear Reader,

After writing Quinn and Maggie's story, *Bordering on Obsession*, I had to give Maggie's best friend, Kimberly, her own book. Production assistant Kimberly Covington is the kind of woman so many of us are: hardworking, practical and longing for wild, lusty sex with just the right guy. So I sent Jason Parker to her, a dangerous man with his own agenda.

A Burning Obsession is part of my HEROES, INC. cross-line Harlequin Intrigue/Blaze series of ex-military men who take on classified missions. While each story can stand alone, I hope you'll look for them all. Next month another HEROES, INC. story, "Touch Me," will be part of a special paranormal anthology titled *Essence of Midnight* that I'm writing with Julie Kenner and Julie Elizabeth Leto. And then watch for more HEROES, INC. Intrigue novels in November and December.

I always enjoy hearing from readers—you can find me on the Internet at SusanKearney.com.

Best,

Susan Kearney

Books by Susan Kearney

HARLEQUIN BLAZE
25—ENSLAVED
50—DOUBLE THE THRILL
96—BORDERING ON OBSESSION

A BURNING OBSESSION
Susan Kearney

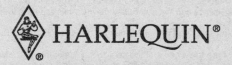 HARLEQUIN®

TORONTO • NEW YORK • LONDON
AMSTERDAM • PARIS • SYDNEY • HAMBURG
STOCKHOLM • ATHENS • TOKYO • MILAN • MADRID
PRAGUE • WARSAW • BUDAPEST • AUCKLAND

For Brenda Chin and Melissa Jeglinski—
thank you both for all the help.

ISBN 0-373-79142-9

A BURNING OBSESSION

Copyright © 2004 by Susan Hope Kearney.

1

"Why is she taking off her clothes?"

Jason Parker peered through the monitor focused on the interior of the public bathroom. The security cameras allowed him to see into the restroom but not beyond the closed stall door.

Kimberly Hayward had just tossed over the door the skin-tight top she'd been wearing, creating an unabashed hunger in Jason to see more of her than her delectable calves and her sensuous feet. If Jason hadn't known better, he might have suspected Kimberly was taunting him, teasing him. Distracting him from his job.

But she couldn't possibly know he was watching. She couldn't know he was on an undercover mission for the Shey Group and that the U.S. government had tagged her for surveillance. Due to the government's priority on stopping terrorism, her case didn't warrant a high enough priority for the authorities to assign an official agent to watch her, so the Shey Group's boss, Logan Kincaid, had pegged Jason for this mission. Only, Jason hadn't expected the task of watching Kimberly Hayward to be so arousing. He shifted in his seat.

For the past week, Kimberly's flirty eyes, her sassy

smile and her look-at-me stride had been driving him crazy. Tonight would probably require another cold shower if he intended to get a lick of sleep.

Not for the first time this week, Jason cursed Logan Kincaid for "volunteering" him for this particular mission—which up until now had required the rudimentary skills of a Peeping Tom. As much as Jason preferred fantasizing about Kimberly's slender body to wondering about her motives, he couldn't help speculating about her peculiar behavior. Why wasn't she strutting down the stacks of library books in search of a good read during their stopover in Cornwall, or using the computer to e-mail back home to the States like every other tourist? He'd like nothing better than to report back to Kincaid that there was nothing unusual in Kimberly's behavior.

But no, she had to slip into the British library and remove her clothes in the lavatory. And her hidden striptease was beating his pulse up another notch.

The library security guard stepped into the office, frowned at the screen and spoke in his crisp English accent. "We don't allow for that sort of behavior in the loo, sir. If she's on holiday and meeting—"

"She isn't." Kimberly had come to Great Britain alone, a trait Jason found both courageous and appealing. In his experience women tended to travel in twos, either pairing up with a man or going to clubs and parties with a girlfriend. That Kimberly was visiting England alone told him she was comfortable in her own skin, quite lovely skin with her smooth southern California tan and… *You're here on business. Get a grip.* Besides, he hadn't seen her talking

with anyone beyond her tour guide or fellow travelers. He doubted she was about to do something deliciously illicit in the library's lavatory.

The guard frowned. "I'll have her removed from the premises."

"Not yet. Maybe she's just changing into another outfit."

At her suspicious antics, Jason's thoughts had shifted from idle to overdrive in two seconds flat. During the past week, he'd watched Kimberly Hayward drink tea in a shimmering dress slit so high above her knee she could have been arrested. He'd watched her toned butt fill out clingy short shorts as she took the steps two at a time at the Tower of London. And he'd seen her sunning on Brighton beach in a mouthwatering bikini. Always fresh-faced and sparkly-eyed, she had an innocent look that a man of Jason's sophisticated tastes rarely saw.

After a week of secretly watching her and waiting for her to make a suspicious move, he'd come to appreciate her slanted green eyes, the angle of her jaw when her curiosity was aroused, and the pursing of her mouth every time she stopped to take a picture. She had kiss-me lips and a cute little nose, but it was her eyes that fascinated him. Irresistible sloping emerald irises that had pitched him a curve ball.

Oh, yeah. He wanted her.

And he didn't know why. His tastes usually inclined toward voluptuous, big-haired women who wore tight clothes, too much makeup and too much jewelry. Women who expected nothing more from him than a good time. Jason liked experienced

women, and until this week he hadn't believed that a fresh-faced, starry-eyed, just-out-of-college girl could heat his interest. But heat it she had—to a boil.

Kimberly flung her skirt over the top of the stall door.

"Look at that, mate." The security guard nodded enthusiastically despite his former utterance of disapproval.

When Jason noted the seam of his jeans pressing into his crotch, he swore. The blond, dewy-eyed California coed was getting to him. Did she wear a thong or white cotton panties? Was her bra a sexy V-cut, satin or lace? Jason's frustration rose along with his erection. He gritted his teeth and shifted his weight again.

Until now, Kimberly had seemed a regular American tourist on a European tour. She hadn't acted suspiciously—at least not since last week when U.S. Customs had caught her going through security with rocks hidden in a padded bra. A dry run, the authorities theorized—in preparation for smuggling. Jason hadn't believed the report. In fact, he thought this entire mission a joke—until now.

When Kimberly draped a sheer white bra over the stall, he swore again and zoomed in on the garment. Small, lacy, feminine. No room for hidden rocks in that scrap of mesh. That a jewel thief of his caliber had been reduced to examining a woman's lingerie didn't sit well with Jason. But a commitment was a commitment. He might be a thief, but he was a man of his word.

Jason had promised Logan Kincaid that he would

repay a big favor, one large enough to keep Jason out of a jail cell. Otherwise, he never would have been here in the first place. So instead of drinking champagne on the French Riviera and hobnobbing with the rich and powerful while he secretly relieved wealthy women of their jewelry, Jason Parker was ogling the wise-eyed American tourist with the golden tan.

That she was standing behind a stall door in just her panties intrigued Jason enough to shove aside his annoyance at his assignment. Besides looking good enough to eat for breakfast, this striptease was the first interesting thing Kimberly had done all week—if he didn't count her spilling tea on an earl during a visit to Dumbroke Palace. She was an inquisitive thing, too, asking her tour guide so many questions that Jason's head spun.

Two minutes passed and Kimberly pulled the clothes back into the stall. Then she opened the door and exited, fully dressed.

"Oh, she's good." Jason muttered.

If he hadn't been a trained observer, if the head of the Shey Group hadn't insisted that the U.S. government considered Kimberly Hayward dangerous, Jason would never have recognized that the sexy blond woman on a vacation tour had ditched the hottie sandals, flirty skirt and spaghetti-strapped midriff-revealing top for a navy business suit with button-down white blouse, horn-rimmed glasses, a brown wig and what he suspected was a padded bra because her chest size had expanded. She stopped in front of the mirror, wiped her pink lipstick from her mouth and straightened her wig, then with brisk steps that

bespoke a woman on a quest, she strode out of the restroom.

Goodbye, carefree tourist. Hello, Madam Serious. With the boldly angled chin and the squared-to-do-battle shoulders of a somber scholar, she'd changed her entire persona. She wasn't just good, she was amazing.

While these clothes weren't as revealing as the ones she'd worn all week, she still projected an unattainable attitude that glued Jason's gaze to the monitor. In stockings her legs looked as they said in the U.K., smashing, and the conservative jacket showed off her nipped-in waist to perfection.

However, Jason's other instincts had just kicked in, too. Suspicious instincts. Until this moment, he hadn't believed that Kimberly Hayward could possibly be the devious spy her government suspected her to be.

But just when he'd concluded that the mission the Shey Group had sent him on was a wild-goose chase meant to torture his libido, his spying was paying off.

Could the sweet-faced girl with the slender body have been fooling him all week? Jason found the unexpected change in her not only unusually fascinating, but compelling. She might even have a talent that paralleled his own light-fingered touch.

And he'd bet the hefty commission that Kincaid insisted on paying him, that Kimberly Hayward was about to get herself invited into the restricted area of the Cornwall library. But why the disguise? What was her goal?

For once, Jason wished he'd paid attention to all of those annoying questions she'd peppered their

guide with. Unless it came to jewelry, he didn't care much about history. However, even he knew that this library housed the *Book of Celts*, a valuable British treasure passed down from the time of the Roman invasion of the British Isles and kept under lock and key, only studied by scholars with the highest of credentials.

On a series of monitors, Jason followed her progress down the hallway. Her flirty walk had disappeared. She now strode in businesslike fashion right past several travelers in her tour group, who never gave her a second glance. Even the man in the baggy surfer shorts named Alex Taylor, who'd kept shyly smiling at Kimberly all week—the man *she* never seemed to notice—hadn't recognized her in her disguise.

Reaching into the large leather satchel where she must have stuffed her extra clothes, Kimberly pulled out a business card and handed it to the library attendant. "Good afternoon," her clear voice, bright and warm as California sunshine, rippled through the microphone. "I'm Dr. Johnson from Stanford University. I have an appointment."

For the second time, the library's security guard, sitting beside Jason, frowned. The guard's hand went to the phone.

Jason clamped a hand over the man's wrist and applied gentle pressure. "Please, allow me to handle this."

"But—"

"If you need permission to follow my lead..." Jason deliberately let his voice trail off. It was rumored

that the head of the Shey Group had tentacles that
extended from all the way inside the White House
and across the Atlantic to the highest members of the
British Parliament. When Jason had first entered the
library, the suspicious guard had called his superiors
for permission to allow the American to use the security system. After several phone calls up the chain
of command, the guard's hostile attitude had done a
one-eighty. Jason didn't know what kind of strings
Kincaid had pulled, but the man had clout with a cap-
ital *C*.

"Dr. Johnson" followed the librarian into a back
room. The librarian donned gloves, removed a key
from her pocket, inserted it into a lock, then rever-
ently removed a leather-bound book.

"Is that the *Book of Celts*?" Jason asked, surprised
that the volume was over four inches thick and at least
two feet high. Too big to hide in Kimberly's leather
satchel and smuggle out of the library. But then again,
she might just be scoping out the locale first before
making her move.

"That's it, all right. The *Book of Celts*."

Jason's eyes narrowed at the dim screen that
showed floor-to-ceiling wood-and-glass cabinets lined
with hundreds of leather volumes. "Can you turn up
the lighting?"

"No, sir. Direct light can damage the pages of
these old books."

Jason watched Kimberly carry the precious artifact
to the farthest table. The librarian left her alone in the
quiet room. With Kimberly's back to the video camera, he couldn't see what she was doing. But the mi-

crophone picked up every sound. The crinkle of pages turning.

Then the unmistakable sound of paper ripping.

The security guard cursed.

Kimberly shoved her hand and a piece of paper under her suit jacket. Jason suspected she'd just ripped a page out of a thousand-year-old book and hidden it under her clothing. She hadn't intended to steal the entire book—just a page, but the action offended Jason's sensibilities. Didn't she realize that she'd just devalued her product by tearing it?

"Is she crazy?" The security guard beside him breathed heavily and rose to his feet. "We can't let her leave the library."

KIMBERLY HAYWARD hadn't tripped or dropped the book or set off any alarms. Her plan to recreate in real time the scene she'd written in her script had gone off like clockwork. She couldn't quite believe it.

She looked right, left, back over her shoulder, but the room was empty. And with her back to the video monitor, even if someone had been watching, they couldn't have seen what she'd done.

Satisfied she'd accomplished her goal, she returned the *Book of Celts* to the librarian and headed back to the ladies' restroom to change. The security monitors would view the same woman walking out who had walked in—a necessary deception in the plot she'd concocted. Soon she'd again be dressed in comfortable clothes and back into tourist mode.

Containing her excitement in a scheme well-

executed, she ordered her feet not to skip. She didn't need to fall on her face and draw attention to herself. The European trip was turning out better than she'd planned.

She was halfway down the dimly lit hallway when a man's arm stretched out from a darkened nook. Strong fingers grabbed her upper arm and yanked her against his chest. A very hard, very forbidding chest.

He clamped a hand over her lips, turning her gasp into a terrified squeal. Frantic, she dropped her satchel, then realized she should have at least tried to hit him with it. Instead, she brought up her knee, aiming for his groin.

"Hey, careful. You could hurt me." Her attacker twisted, and her blow glanced harmlessly off a muscular thigh.

Damn.

He'd spoken with an American accent, and she forced her head up to look at his face. He had black, short hair, dark blue eyes, the brows arched almost in amusement. His jaw was wide, neatly shaved and his lips were full and mocking. And he wore an immaculate gray suit, white shirt and tie, not the usual uniform of a criminal, but then again, he was holding her so tightly, he was cutting off the circulation to her brain.

She couldn't think clearly but that didn't deter her. She raised her fists to strike his throat, and he grabbed both her wrists in one hand and pinned her up against him. Then he swiveled, trapping her between his body and the wall and covered her mouth with his hand.

"I won't hurt you."

Yeah, right.

"If I let go of your mouth, will you promise not to scream?" His voice was cool and controlled, almost polite, but the sound hissed through her like a hot knife.

If he hadn't been holding her up, her watery knees might have given way. Not just because of the fear shooting through her, but because she was thinking the man with Mel Gibson eyes should make his living as a soap star instead of assaulting women in libraries. Kimberly's work as an assistant producer at Simitar Studios brought her into close contact with many celebrities. Good looks didn't bowl her over. But she didn't expect to meet an American in England with such rugged handsomeness and the body of an action hero...who the hell was he?

Not a mugger. He hadn't hurt her.

Not a thief. He hadn't gone for her purse.

As close as he held her, he had to feel her trembling. She nodded that she wouldn't scream.

"I'll take that for a *yes.*" He removed his hand from her mouth but kept her wrists pinned over her head.

Oh, God. Her only knowledge of dealing with the illegal mind came from research she'd done for her script. Showing fear was bad. And making eye contact established a rapport that was supposed to make it more difficult for him to harm her. Looking into those gorgeous baby blues under normal circumstances wouldn't have been a hardship. But her brain was having trouble classifying such a gorgeous male specimen as a criminal. Still, those massive muscles

presented a danger. His tight grip on her reminded her that certain serial killers had devastating smiles. Ted Bundy came to mind. The idea that this man could cut off her scream and keep her pinned to the wall, had fear sucking all the moisture from her mouth.

"What do you want?"

"The page you ripped from the *Book of Celts.*"

Oh, God. He wasn't a rapist or a murderer. He probably worked for the library. He thought...he thought she'd ripped a page from the book. "You don't understand—"

"Enlighten me." He leaned in, wedging her spine even tighter against the wall, using his sheer strength to threaten her.

"I'm Kimberly Hayward and I—"

"You just told the librarian that you're Dr. Johnson."

He'd been watching her. Eavesdropping on her conversation. Yet she'd never suspected. The tight press of his massive chest against her made her lightheaded. "Please, I can't breathe."

"Talk to me, doll baby."

"My name is really Kimberly. Kimberly Hayward."

"Not Dr. Johnson?"

She shook her head. One side of his well-proportioned mouth curled up in amusement.

"Are you security?" She suspected if he'd been going to hurt her, he'd already have done so. She tried not to think about what else he could want from her.

"I'm asking the questions, lady." He lowered his voice to a silky whisper threaded with steel.

"Okay. Okay." He'd just asked her something. But she couldn't remember the question. She needed air. She couldn't think with that big body pressing against her. She licked her lips. "What's the question again?"

He chuckled, the tone of his laughter perfect for a leading man. "You're some piece of work. Did you think you could just prance in here and steal a valuable artifact?"

"I didn't *steal* anything. I'm a production assistant for Simitar Studios."

"Yeah, right." He tapped the pad of one finger on her skin, right in the V of her bra. Her bra?

Oh, my God.

While they'd been talking, his clever fingers had somehow bypassed her jacket and unbuttoned her blouse. And she'd never noticed.

Now aware of his fingers under her shirt, skimming across her bra's padding, she realized that just one tiny plastic clip stood between his fingers and her being topless. Not that she had a lot to hide—but that wasn't the point. Her vulnerability had her forgetting everything, except what he was about to do next.

"What are you doing?"

"Looking for evidence."

Lightly, he ran his fingers over the padded cups, and, although the padding was thick, so that when she hid papers inside the secret compartment they wouldn't show, she was excruciatingly aware of her tender and vulnerable flesh just below his fingers.

Now seemed like the right time to scream for help.

As if reading her mind, he clamped one thick palm over her mouth once more, and she never got a chance to release the scream she'd been saving up. And then his fingers found the secret compartment in the bra, extracted the paper she'd just hidden there.

That he was more interested in the paper he'd found than in her breasts should have reassured her. But she'd just traded one problem for another.

"And what have we here?" He flicked his wrist, unfolding the rumpled paper. His attention concentrated on his find, and his blue eyes narrowed. "A fish and chips receipt? What the hell?"

"Mmm." She tried to speak.

He released her mouth. He had the oddest expression in his eyes. Bright. Amused. "Talk to me, lady. And leave out the BS."

"I'm researching a script."

"And I'm Arnold Schwarzenegger."

"Actually, you'd make a better Mel Gibson."

"Answer my question."

"I think better when I can breathe."

He eased up the pressure. "Talk."

She wanted to button her blouse. She wanted to scream. But mostly she wanted to slap her boss Quinn Scott for putting her in this position. Luckily for him, Quinn was off on his honeymoon with Kimberly's best friend Maggie, his happy bride, so she took out her aggravation on the nearest target. Her captor.

"You idiot." Now, insulting him was dumb, but Kimberly barely stopped to think. Perhaps it had been his chuckle or his smile or those cool baby blues that

made her believe this man wasn't about to hurt her. But all that built-up anxiety needed release and merged into an explosion of frustration. "I'm researching a script for Quinn Scott."

"And he asked you to steal a page from the *Book of Celts*?"

"Don't be stupid. You know that I didn't steal anything."

"Careful of the names you call me. I haven't checked your panties, yet."

She glared at him. "There's nothing in them that would interest you."

"Don't be so sure."

She didn't know how to respond to his obvious and inappropriate innuendo, so she just scowled and stared over his right shoulder, praying someone would wander down the hall. Praying that somehow she would get through the next few minutes and that doing so would give her the courage to continue with her plans, she swallowed back a smart retort. How was she going to recreate the next scenes in her script if she couldn't deal with one man in the hall of a public library? Where were all the tourists in her group when she needed them?

Apparently, Mr. Too-Beautiful didn't like being ignored. He tilted up her chin, forcing her gaze to him. His hand was warm, his fingers gentle, yet exerting just enough pressure that she didn't quite dare pull away.

"Why did you tell the librarian that you were Dr. Johnson?" he demanded.

"So I could examine the book—not steal it or rip

pages out of it." When he didn't release her, she raised her voice. "Didn't you hear me? I said I came to *examine* it."

"Why?"

"I already told you I'm doing research, although it's none of your business."

"I'm making it my business." He leaned against her again. And with her blouse open, he seemed so much closer, bigger. Sexier.

But the dangerous glimmer in his pupils warned her not to toy with the man.

She tossed her hair out of her eyes, drawing courage from someplace she hadn't known existed. "You aren't going to believe me."

"Probably not."

She expelled a long sigh. "So just let me go, and we can forget this ever happened." Like she'd ever forget this moment. She'd probably have dreams about him for weeks. Just her luck that the most interesting man she'd ever met was probably going to turn her over to the police.

"Quit stalling. I want an explanation for your suspicious behavior."

"Sheesh. Don't you ever listen? I'm researching a screenplay."

"Of course you are."

Obviously, he didn't believe her and that's why he kept asking the same question. She'd learned a long time ago there was no point in arguing with stupid people because they could never see any point but their own. She didn't know why she was explaining. Except she was scared and intrigued, and half-dressed

and being held much too closely by the handsome stranger to think clearly. But of one thing she was sure. The faster she talked, the faster he'd release her.

And she really needed him to let her go, because her body wasn't reacting to this man as the threat he was. Oh no. Her olfactory nerves liked the scent of his spicy soap. Her traitorous eyes couldn't seem to stop staring into his. And worst of all, beneath her padded bra—her nipples were tight and hard.

"My boss is willing to greenlight—"

"Greenlight?"

"Go ahead on my project, but first he wants certain details authenticated."

"What kind of details?"

Since Mr. Gorgeous was still holding her hostage against the wall, she most certainly was not about to tell him that Quinn Scott had decided her thriller should have erotic elements. The famous screenwriter, director and producer had actually gone through her story and demanded that she add sex scenes—sex scenes so racy she hadn't yet figured out how to write them. In addition, Quinn had dared her to verify that every heist and every murder could really be pulled off because he wanted reality. Demanded authentication. And then Maggie, with a twinkle in her eyes, had dared Kimberly to come up with exotic and erotic love scenes that would match the intensity of the suspense. During a phone call, Kimberly had mentioned Maggie's suggestion to another friend, Cate, who thought the idea wonderful—easy for them to suggest from the safety of their homes.

Kimberly had started with the suspense element, making sure her plan to have her characters steal a page from the well-guarded *Book of Celts* would work. She still didn't know how she was going to write all the erotic scenes the writer/producer had asked her to add to the script. Then Maggie had dared her to verify those as yet unwritten love scenes, too, and the idea warmed Kimberly straight to her toes every time she considered the idea. And she had an entire suitcase back in her hotel room packed full of sexy costumes to help her get into the mood—a suitcase she'd barely opened, except to remove the wig and padded bra.

"The script calls for the heroine to wear a special undergarment with a hidden pouch."

"Like the one you're wearing?" His glance dropped to her bra.

"Exactly." She spoke boldly, as if her state of undress didn't bother her, but a betraying blush crept up her neck and heated her cheeks.

"Let me see if I have this straight. You wrote a movie—"

"Screenplay."

"And your boss Quinn Scott, who is almost as famous as Steven Spielberg, wants you to verify the details. And one of those details is stealing a page from the *Book of Celts*."

"You get an A-plus." She shoved against him, hoping he'd loosen his grip. He didn't budge one inch.

"Lady—"

"Kimberly."

"—that is the most ridiculous story I've ever heard. I suppose Quinn Scott will verify—"

Uh-oh. "He's in Tahiti."

"Maybe his secretary can—"

Double uh-oh. "He married his secretary and she's with him."

"So we can call them and verify your story?"

"The island is private and there are no phones."

Even Kimberly realized how perfectly absurd her story sounded. But Quinn and Maggie had wanted to be alone, incommunicado, they'd gone to an island where no reporters could find them, where no studio emergency could interrupt their honeymoon. Kimberly figured her captor was about to march her down to the local police station, and she'd have to go through her explanation all over again. Her face flushed even hotter at the idea of having to describe to a roomful of cops that her boss had paid for her to tour Great Britain to research the theft of national treasures which required hiding them inside her padded bra.

"Look. Why don't you check the *Book of Celts*? The librarian has it under lock and key. The book is undamaged. I didn't do anything wrong."

With no warning, the man holding her let her go.

Kimberly didn't wait around to press her luck. She shouldered past him and sprinted to the restroom. After taking several deep breaths, she forced herself to finish her task, and change from her disguise back into Kimberly the tourist, so her fellow sightseers wouldn't be suspicious. With shaking fingers, she removed her now-wrinkled suit, padded bra and wig.

Once she was again wearing her regular clothes, she steadied. Her nightmarish encounter no longer seemed quite so real. Mr. Pretty Blue Eyes couldn't have been that attractive. He couldn't have undressed her without her noticing him unfastening her buttons. She'd just been too frightened to notice.

That's when she glanced in the mirror and took note of her flushed face and messy hair. She didn't exactly look as though she'd just survived a tussle with a stranger. She looked like a woman who'd recently left a lover. Her eyes were dilated and her belly was tight with the aftereffects of his restraining her.

Kimberly splashed water on her face. Brushed her hair. And tried hard not to think about Mr. Perfect.

She couldn't let the incident dissuade her from following through on her project. After years of film school and writing screenplay after screenplay while working two jobs, last year she'd finally landed a job at Simitar Studios as one of Quinn's production assistants.

And the famous writer/director/producer had read her script and was ready to make an offer on her first sale. She was so close to success that determination washed away her fear. Somehow she would complete the job she'd come here to do—theft scenes and murder scenes would all be thoroughly checked for authenticity. The duplication needn't be completely real. She wasn't going to really murder or really steal—just reenact them as closely as possible. And somehow, she would have to dredge up some wonderfully exciting love scenes.

On those love scenes, Kimberly kept drawing a

blank. Between Maggie and Quinn's wedding, and all the tasks she'd had to complete before the couple had left, she'd had no time to write. She'd slept on the flight over the Atlantic and arrived too jet-lagged to focus. Okay, that was an excuse. She was putting off writing the love scenes. Although she had a vivid imagination, she couldn't get in the right mood and hoped the new scenery would stimulate her creativity. Kimberly had no trouble writing murder and mayhem and thievery, but when it came to erotic encounters, she was at a loss. But she would not fail in her assignment.

She'd come too far, worked too hard to turn tail and run home. Lots of production assistants never got the shot she was getting. Still when she'd asked Quinn to read her script she'd never imagined she'd have to go to these kinds of extremes to sell her project. Although she'd figured out how to commit "pretend" murders and "fake" thefts, she still had no idea what to write for those hot love scenes.

A sexy lover to put her in the mood would have come in handy this summer. She dated occasionally but there was no one special in her life, so there'd been no one to ask to accompany her on this working European vacation. She spent too many hours at work to have much time for a social life. And the people she met on the set or in the office tended to be just as driven as she was.

But Kimberly didn't regret one minute she'd spent running errands for demanding directors, reading screenplays recommended by the studio's first readers or making sure Quinn's latest star had the chocolate

biscotti she craved with her morning latte. Hundreds of thousands of wannabe writers would give anything to be in her position, on the verge of earning six figures and seeing their script on the big screen. She ought to know: as Quinn's production assistant, her job required her to write coverage on at least four scripts a week, most of which were okay, just not good enough to make the final cut. If not for her work as a production assistant, Kimberly would never have met Maggie or Quinn Scott. Now he'd read her script. Even though he'd requested the addition of those love scenes, Quinn wouldn't have given her revisions or paid for this trip if he didn't intend to produce it. She was going to make the most of the opportunity her boss had thrown her way—thanks to his new wife, Maggie.

Kimberly wished she could phone Maggie or Cate now, but with Maggie out of touch in Tahiti on her honeymoon and Cate always working, she couldn't reach either of them. Maggie and Quinn weren't even due back in L.A. until the end of the month—the time limit Quinn had given her to complete her task.

Too bad Maggie hadn't asked her husband to assign one of Simitar Studio's hunky male actors to accompany Kimberly and help her slip into the right frame of mind to write those love scenes—an actor like the good-looking security guard who'd felt her up? Yeah, right. Kimberly chuckled at the thought. Maggie was the one with the outrageous schemes. Thanks to Kimberly's dare to make a major change in her life, Maggie had seduced Quinn on their very first date. Kimberly couldn't help but wonder if

Quinn's request to add those love scenes was done at Maggie's goading.

However, after Kimberly's encounter with that yummy guard, her creative juices were flowing, and she envisioned the characters in her script sharing hot kisses, frenzied caresses. Even now, her pulse still hadn't settled and she walked with an extra spring in her step, a warmth between her thighs that unnerved her. The man was a stranger and yet she'd responded to him as if…

Don't go there.

Kimberly left the library and brought a Cornish pasty from a local bakery, hoping the hot treat would calm her. She ate the steak-and-potato and cheese delicacy as she strode down the cobblestone street and headed back to the hotel. Somewhere between her close call at the library and her discovery that a cruise ship had anchored and dropped thousands of tourists into the narrow streets of Cornwall, her urge to explore the seaside town had vanished.

One of the reasons Quinn had chosen this particular tour for her, besides the fact that it covered every city mentioned in the script, was that it gave her lots of free time to explore on her own. The group rode together by bus and van or train, a knowledgeable guide helping them along the way, but once quartered in a cozy hotel, she was free to play out the scenarios in her script uninterrupted. At least usually.

The hot pasty did nothing to calm her previous tension from her encounter with the guard. Kimberly likely wouldn't regain her equilibrium until she had four solid walls around her again. Finally, next to the

antique shop with silver-handled walking canes in the window, she spotted the scenic hotel with welcoming baskets of flowers on both sides of the front door and jogged up the steps two at a time.

Her eyes took a moment to adjust from the bright daylight outside to the dim interior. Her tour guide, Liam Short stood in the reception area and shot her a friendly wave. "Kimberly, we've picked up another traveler. I'd like you to meet—"

No. It couldn't be him.

"—Jason Parker."

Not Mr. I could be a movie star but I'd rather accost American tourists in the library.

"He's going to be spending the next few weeks with our group."

Floored, Kimberly stared at the man who'd questioned her and undressed her in the library. He looked too big for the crowded lobby. Too handsome. Too in-charge. What was he doing here and how had he beaten her to the hotel? And how had he known where she was staying?

Jason Parker's sudden joining of their group couldn't be accidental. He looked way too pleased with himself and his oh-so-blue eyes sported a definite twinkle, almost as if he knew that her mouth had gone dry and her nipples had immediately hardened at the sight of him. And then to cap it off, he actually winked at her.

"Kimberly and I bumped into one another in the library."

Bumped!

Liam spoke in his Irish brogue. "Ah, then you have

a love of reading in common. I'll be sure to sit you two together for dinner.''

Had he really had the nerve to say *bumped?*

Kimberly battled down anger—at least enough to speak through her haze of red. ''We will not sit together during dinner. This man's a criminal. You should call the police.''

2

JASON GRINNED, just to irritate her. After all, irritating her seemed only fair after the way her green eyes heated him up like a frisky stallion. "Calling the police would be inappropriate."

"Really? Wouldn't that be like letting a criminal tell the judge what his sentence should be?" Kimberly countered, her tone revealing that she was quite miffed with him.

Her insinuation about criminals hit just a little too close to home, and Jason took care not to react to her comment. Whoever had said that women looked beautiful when angry had never faced Kimberly Hayward's wrath. She didn't just glower at him, she stomped over, speaking as she took those long-legged strides, looking about as adorable as a tigress on the hunt. Then she stabbed her pointing finger in his chest. "This man accosted me."

She'd spoken loudly enough to turn the heads of other curious hotel guests. Jason chuckled, just to irritate her even more. "If I hadn't stopped you, the security guard would have and he wouldn't have been as nice."

Kimberly's eyes smoldered with fury. "Nice?"

Liam looked from Kimberly to Jason in confusion. "Security guard?"

Apparently Kimberly didn't feel up to enlightening him. She compressed her lips, pivoted on her heel and stormed up the stairs, muttering, "Nice men don't feel up women they don't know while they pin them to the wall."

"Don't worry. I'll smooth things over," Jason told the puzzled guide. "It's just a little spat between friends. Good friends." He gave the impression that he and Kimberly were intimately acquainted, and the guide grinned back, sharing a glance of unspoken understanding that men can never expect women to act logically.

When the other hotel guests realized the fireworks had ended, they moved on, but not before several ladies, who apparently hadn't believed Kimberly's accusation, made it known by encouraging smiles that they would welcome his attention. However, one older woman gave him a wide berth as he followed Kimberly up the stairs.

He knocked on the door she'd just slammed.

"Liam?"

"It's Jason."

"I don't know anyone named Jason," Kimberly yelled through the door.

"That's because I didn't introduce myself properly at the library."

"I doubt you know how to do anything properly," Kimberly countered, in a voice so annoyed that Jason chuckled again. She was more correct than she'd known. He might have been brought up in the best

of homes, but Jason had spent the last ten years building his wealth. To him, prosperity was a smoke screen to mask his illegal activities.

What he lacked in morality, he made up for with charm, charm he intended to use on Miss Kimberly. Although his usual tastes ran to flashier women, he liked Kimberly's looks, her spunk and independent nature. Actually there was nothing he disliked about her—except the fact that she might be a spy. But just because her parents had been spies didn't mean that she had followed in their footsteps. After all, Jason's folks were upstanding Bostonians who would be appalled by their son's chosen career. So while Jason didn't know the real Kimberly, he wasn't about to believe unsubstantiated accusations. While eventually he intended to get to the bottom of this puzzle, he fully intended to take his time and enjoy the process.

"Look, we're going to be traveling together for the next week or so."

"Not if I have you arrested."

"Please, open your door. I came to apologize."

"For assaulting and undressing me?"

He'd barely touched her. And he suspected her anger was because he'd caught her in the act—but in the act of what, he still wasn't sure. While her story made sense in a convoluted way, it wasn't the perfect cover. A real thief would have come up with a better story, one that could be easily verified. However, he no longer saw a reason to follow her secretly. Not when it was so much more convenient to keep a close eye on her by joining her tour group.

Instead of watching her from a discreet distance,

he could sit next to her on the train and enjoy her conversation as well as her delicate citrus scent. He could glance at her across the dinner table and watch her delectable lips. And he could most definitely make opportunities to flirt and tease.

"It's difficult to apologize through this door."

"And I'd have to be crazy to open my door for you."

Talking was getting him nowhere. Jason reached into his pocket, snapped open his tool set and picked her lock in mere seconds. He opened her door, which didn't have one of those useless little chains like those in American hotels, stepped inside and closed it behind him.

A flowerpot sailed through the air at his head. She had a good arm. He ducked, the ceramic pot crashed against the door and dirt scattered across the oak floor.

Before she could launch another missile at him or shout for help, Jason lunged across the room, grabbed Kimberly's wrists and dumped her onto the queen-size bed. He sprawled on top of her, enjoying the feel of her lithe curves pressed against his. Obviously she hadn't a clue what all her squirming was doing to him, but in such an intimate position, she'd find out real soon if they'd remained this close.

When she opened her mouth to scream, her eyes more angry than frightened, he shook his head. "Don't scream or—"

"Or what? You'll clamp your filthy hand over my mouth, again?"

His hands were immaculate. He didn't need to look

to know. A thief required a sensitive touch to pick different kinds of locks. Nor could a thief afford a rough nail that might catch on a tool at a critical moment. Jason kept his hands in top-notch condition.

"If you don't like my hands, perhaps you would prefer that I kissed you quiet?"

"Oh, please." She twisted her strong yet sensual body in an attempt to dislodge him, but his thighs settled firmly between her strong legs that cradled him as if they were an ideal fit. Perfectly proportioned, her hips were narrow, her waist slender and her lovely breasts revealed tight hard nipples that suggested she might not object to him so very much after all.

He remembered her reaction to him at the library, the feel of her skin all trembly and smooth beneath the pad of his fingertip. The way her lips pressed together whenever she was thinking hard. The way her hips wriggled against him.

With her violent twisting and turning beneath him right now, he feared she'd hurt herself. But he also knew that her fiery movements were creating havoc with his senses. Didn't she have any idea how good her breasts felt against his chest? If she didn't hold still, he wouldn't be able to contain his arousal.

They were in a hotel room, on a bed. He could have her undressed in less than five seconds and then he could nibble a sleek path down here neck. Feast on her mouth. Savor...no he shouldn't.

He spoke through gritted teeth. "Stop thrashing."

She panted. With her hair fanned out around her head, her eyes looked too big for her face. "Let me go."

"We need to talk."

"I'm not interested in anything you have to say."

"If you don't want to talk, can I assume that all your thrashing around is simply foreplay?"

Her eyes flashed with anger. She leaned forward and bit his shoulder. No love bite. Pain careened down his arm, and he cursed, but he didn't let her go. "If you try that again, I'll tie you up with the drapery cords."

At his threat, she stilled. Her eyes widened and she panted from her exertions.

"That's better." He released her hands, stood, walked to the other side of the room and leaned his back against the door. While he still blocked her escape, he gave her all the room he could. "I don't want to hurt you."

"I feel so much better now," she muttered sarcastically, leaping off the bed as if the mattress were in flames.

"I'm the only one here who got hurt." He rubbed his sore shoulder, wondering if her teeth would leave a permanent bite mark. For some reason wearing her brand didn't bother him. In fact, he rather liked the idea, but knew better than to say so. "I might be bleeding."

"Now, you want me to feel sorry for you? You barged into my room. You can just turn around and barge your way out."

He admired her sassy attitude, but he wasn't going anywhere. Not when he was having so much fun. Not before he'd done what he'd come to do. With her blond hair once again tangled, her eyes drawn to-

gether in a frown of disapproval and her lips set so tightly against him, he had to look away to refrain from grinning—an act he was positive that she wouldn't appreciate.

Her room was a mess, with books and magazines flung everywhere. The trash overflowed with balled-up pieces of paper. She had sticky notes stuck to her dresser, her closet and her laptop computer. She claimed to be a screenwriter and her room certainly backed up her story.

"I'm not going anywhere—not yet." Jason knew that Kimberly Hayward actually had a genuine job in Hollywood as Quinn Scott's production assistant. She'd even gone to film school. But Logan Kincaid's government contacts believed that her job was a brilliant cover.

Jason thought Kimberly Hayward was exactly what she seemed—until he remembered how easily she'd slipped into the role of Dr. Johnson back at the library. Maybe a spy could have pulled off that kind of deception, but an experienced spy wouldn't have been as frightened as she'd seemed and would have had a verifiable story. But then, maybe she'd feigned the fear and the innocence to throw him off.

"If I ran into the bathroom and locked that door, you'd pick that lock, too, wouldn't you?" She scowled at him, edged toward the fireplace and picked up the poker. Holding the weapon, one that he could easily take away from her, seemed to feed her courage. "Who are you? Why have you been watching me, and why won't you leave me alone?"

"Quinn sent me." Jason was a very good liar, but this was one whopper of a tale.

Her eyes narrowed. "At the library you acted as if you'd never heard of Quinn Scott."

"I lied. I'm a movie consultant and I'm supposed to be making sure you follow through on your assignment." Jason shrugged, careful to portray an I-don't-care-if-you-believe-me-or-not demeanor. "You can call Quinn to check my story if—"

"Like I'm going to believe you, with Quinn so conveniently out of touch on his honeymoon—and I told you that, remember?"

"True."

"Why did you accost me at the library?"

"It was either me or the real security guard. He saw you on the video camera and was ready to call the police."

Her grip tightened on the poker. "And you were with him because?"

"I have to report to Quinn whether or not you can pull off your capers."

Her eyes narrowed. "If you work for Quinn, how come I've never heard of you?"

"I work for his foreign division."

"You have any proof?"

Thankful for the fake cover that included an office and secretary that the Shey Group had set up for him, Jason was ready for her to check out his story. He reached into his pocket, pulled out his wallet and extracted a business card. "You can make the appropriate phone call and verify my connections to the studio, okay?"

She didn't take the card, didn't risk coming closer. "So if Quinn hired you, why did you ask me all those questions at the library?"

"For the security guard's sake." Jason placed the card on the dresser. "The guard was watching us on the hallway monitor. I had to ask questions that would satisfy him."

He wondered if she was going to buy his outrageous story. According to the file that Kincaid had given him, she was accustomed to excessive Hollywood types, but she also had a good mind. Jason relaxed against the door, thoroughly enjoying the challenge of watching her try to trip him up.

"The security guard just let you in?"

"Using a business card and your boss's name does wonders. And security had the best view of the ladies' room," he teased.

"You watched…"

"To both our disappointment, we couldn't see beyond the stall door."

She most obviously didn't want to think about that statement and moved on, her tone hostile and suspicious. "Quinn really sent you?"

"Yes."

"Doesn't he trust me?"

Although Jason had pretended to know nothing of Kimberly's work for Quinn Scott to see if he could break her cover, he knew much more about her than he'd let on.

Kincaid had provided Jason with a copy of her script. More importantly, the Shey Group had bugged Quinn's office, and Jason had read transcripts of the

conversation where Quinn had asked Kimberly to re-
vise the script. But when he'd broken into Kimberly's
room last week in Brighton and found her note to
herself that said, ''find a man to help with love
scenes,'' that made him well prepared to lie again.
''Maggie figured you'd need a partner to help you
work out the sex scenes.''

''What?'' Her eyes went huge with horror and embarrassment and a few other emotions he couldn't
read. But he could guess. She most definitely didn't
like Jason's most brilliant idea. He could live with
her annoyance—just not with her rejection. Kimberly
had a quality about her that made this crazy favor he
was doing for the Shey Group quite pleasurable. In
fact, if he'd known working on this side of the law
could be this challenging and engaging, he might
have switched sides a long time ago.

Jason was having fun pushing her buttons, figuring
it was only fair since she'd pushed so many of his.
''Quinn claims you're so uptight about sex that—''

''Quinn talked to you about my sex life! Quinn?''
Kimberly took a step forward and raised the poker as
if to strike.

Apparently, Jason had made a mistake. She and
Quinn weren't that close. He must have forgotten
something—ah yes, the new wife was the one who'd
made a private comment to her husband, not the other
way around.

''Maggie—''

''Maggie would never betray my confidences.''

Jason knew when he'd hit gold and his stab in the

dark had produced twenty-four carats. "Maggie wants you to be as happy as she is."

"And she chose *you?*" Kimberly shook her head, her eyes rolling toward the ceiling in disbelief. "And didn't say a word to me?"

"Look, I don't know what went on between the bride and groom, I just know that after Quinn's phone call I got an all-expense paid ticket—"

"How come you didn't fly over with me?" Kimberly still held the poker, but at a less threatening angle.

Jason couldn't tell her that he'd been spying on her for the last week. "I had other commitments and flew in from Barcelona. I thought I'd made myself available in plenty of time."

"How do you know Quinn?"

"He brought me in to consult on *Thief of Hearts.*" Jason used the cover the Shey team had supplied for him. But he had actually seen the film and been impressed with the research. A pro had advised the movie people how to go about breaking into the Parisian safe.

"I provided technical help. Just like I can help you with those sex—love—" he amended "—scenes."

Eyes throwing daggers at him, she pointed the poker at the door. "Get out."

"Don't you like me?"

"I don't know you."

"We can get to know one another better. Much better."

Her fingers tensed around the poker. "You're insane."

"You'll get used to me."

"Don't count on it."

He kept the grin from his lips. She hadn't said no. She hadn't tried to separate his head from his shoulders by swinging that poker. She looked from the business card back to him, clearly considering.

His story was far-fetched, but he'd given her enough insider facts to make her consider it. Thanks to the Shey Group's cover and Intel, Jason had the inside scoop on private details of Kimberly's life. But what he really wanted to know wasn't in the files.

However, she was sending subtle signals his way that filled him with hope. The intriguing blush that rose up her neck and pinkened her cheeks, the flare of her nostrils, the rapid pulse beating in her graceful neck gave him cause to believe that the attraction wasn't all one way.

He used his best coaxing tone. "When Quinn sent me on this mission, I had reservations, too. But I find you attractive."

"Oh, that makes everything just fine then."

"And I adore the way you blush. Women so rarely blush anymore." Certainly not the experienced women that he normally pursued. At his words, her blush deepened. He raised one eyebrow, bracing for the eruption.

He didn't have to wait long.

"Go to hell."

Jason turned around, opened her door, stepped through, then spoke calmly. "See you at dinner." He went down the stairs whistling.

He didn't even wince at the sound of the poker striking the door.

AFTER KIMBERLY threw the poker, she wanted to shove her fist through Jason Parker's face. But he hadn't stuck around to brave her rage. Oh, no. The coward had departed—whistling no less.

Oh, God. What the hell was she going to do?

Until now, she'd always liked and admired her boss. But to think that Quinn had fixed her up with that…that…gigolo was so embarrassing that Kimberly wanted to scream and pound her fists on the floor like a two-year-old throwing a temper tantrum.

Of all the nerve. And what hurt the most was that both Quinn and Maggie *knew* that Kimberly had no one to help her with the love scenes. Nor was she likely to find someone. That's probably why she'd omitted those scenes from her final version of the story. But Quinn wanted a sexier version and what Quinn wanted, Quinn got. And once the famous producer had decided he wanted Maggie, her friend hadn't stood a chance of resisting him—although she'd put up quite a fight.

However, Kimberly wasn't bold in the men department. In fact, she tended to be clumsy due to her nervousness. She recalled spilling her tea on the earl, her latest bumbling act in a lifetime of humiliating moments. Unlike Quinn, who'd been born in L.A. and had cut his teeth among Hollywood's elite, she came from a small town and tended to be overwhelmed with big-city attitudes. And the anything-goes Hollywood morality often shocked her midwestern sensibilities.

"Oh, my God." She sank onto the bed, pulled her

legs to her chest and rocked. Now that her anger had moved aside and made way for reason, she understood exactly why Quinn and Maggie had sent Jason to her without telling her up front. First, although he was a handsome man who any woman would find attractive and Kimberly certainly wasn't immune to his uncommon looks, she would have protested out of pride and outrage. Second, as a foreign film consultant, they likely had few friends or associates in common besides Quinn and Maggie. She could spill an entire dinner on him, step all over his feet while dancing, and no one at home would ever know. Third and best of all, after this tour, Kimberly would probably never see him again. Unlike the characters in her screenplay, love needn't be involved in the scenes she acted out.

This was her chance. If she dared to take it.

Kimberly's chance to do something wild and crazy with an absolute stranger. A safe stranger—because Quinn knew Jason. Kimberly had never had a better opportunity to have wild, lusty, smutty sex with so little risk of repercussions. So what if Kimberly never picked up strangers? So what if she didn't do one-night stands? So what if she believed that a man should be her friend before they made love?

Jason was charming, intelligent, sexy, and she'd felt a magnetic pull toward him from the moment they'd met. The mystery of him, the male charisma, the idea of boldly taking what he offered had her wondering if she'd lost her mind.

But this was her shot to break out of her mold as

Maggie had done so successfully. Ah, she was so tempted.

She supposed her take on relationship building came from her parents who had had a great marriage. Her mom and dad had been best friends who did everything together. They'd met in high school, attended college together, married and then had worked together for the CIA. They'd died together in a scuba-diving "accident." She didn't believe the CIA version, but asking questions wouldn't have brought them back, so she'd accepted the official story, done her grieving and moved on with her life. But she'd never stopped wondering....

While her parents had been alive, neither of them would ever have considered going on separate vacations. They'd shared the same friends, played doubles tennis on the same team and even loved the same kinds of spicy foods.

Kimberly had just assumed she'd find a relationship like the one her parents had shared—but it hadn't happened. She'd gotten rid of her virginity during college and been disappointed by both Charlie Phelps and the fact that she'd settled for less than the whole package. She'd tried again two years ago, with Terrence who'd been great in bed, but the lack of shared interests had led to a parting of the ways. He'd liked beer and football. She wanted to talk about books and movies. But at least she'd learned that she wasn't frigid. In fact, she liked sex. But she was picky. Maybe too picky.

This might be a once-in-forever opportunity. Her

chance to let go of practical Kimberly and reach for hot, sweaty, fun that was sure to get her creative juices flowing. Jason Parker might be just the man to turn up the spark in her love scenes as well as in her life.

Jason had super potential. The way he'd asked her those questions in the library to throw off security proved he was clever. And those blue eyes of his fascinated her. So did his amused take on almost every situation.

Kimberly might not be a woman of vast experience but the attraction between them had set off sparks with the promise of combustion. The problem was that she wasn't even sure she liked the man beyond a physical response.

And she couldn't quite believe that she was seriously considering him as a sexual partner. Not sensible, practical Kimberly. She wished she could blame her interest in him on her job. But her interest in the man was so much more than a hope he'd stimulate romantic ideas for her script. Maybe it was leaving home soil, maybe Europe was opening her up to the idea of new experiences, or maybe it was simply that after watching Maggie find happiness, she wanted to go after that kind of happiness herself. Whatever the reason, Jason Parker excited her, intrigued her.

Walking over to the dresser, she stared at the business card. Her parents had often used fake cards on their secret missions. For twenty dollars anyone could give the impression they were something they were not. She would check out his story and go from there. How far she would go, not even she knew.

She dialed the phone and a secretary answered, "British Consulting, Limited."

"Jason Parker, please."

"He's currently on assignment. Would you like to leave a message?"

"This is Kimberly Hayward, Quinn Scott's production assistant. Can you tell me if Jason Parker is working for Simitar Studios?"

"Yes, he is."

So he'd been telling the truth. With a thank-you and a shaking hand, Kimberly put the phone back in the cradle.

The idea of taking Jason up on his offer appealed to her on levels she didn't want to examine too closely. *This was her chance.* A gamble of a lifetime. Hollywood was all about taking gambles. Kimberly didn't want to sell just one script, she wanted a career. She wanted to write and direct. To achieve her goal, she'd left her family and friends behind, gambled that she could begin a new life and she'd succeeded up to a point. Was it time to throw caution to the winds once again?

She wanted to do just that. Which was exactly why she *would* make herself think through her actions. Although she now realized that her heart had never been involved in her past relationships, each time she'd believed she'd been in love. Instead, she'd been in love with the idea of being in love.

Lately, Kimberly had begun to wonder if the capacity to get that giddy feeling that other women seemed to feel about men wasn't in her. She'd never

had that special awareness of a man. Never waited anxiously by the phone hoping it would ring. But maybe she just hadn't found the right guy.

She had no deep internal scars that prevented her from falling in love. Barring the scuba-diving "accident" that had claimed her parents' lives two weeks after she'd graduated from high school, her family background was as close to ideal as it could be. When she'd been little, her parents had taken her with them on several missions. When she'd been older, they sometimes had to leave her behind with her aunt, but never for long. She'd suffered no childhood traumas. Her parents had loved her.

So why hadn't she ever fallen in love? At age twenty-six, she had to look internally for the reasons. Was she looking for perfection? For a soul mate who didn't exist?

She wouldn't jump into bed with a man unless she'd considered all the angles—one of which had to be getting to know the man better. She didn't know anything about Jason, but he'd certainly grabbed her attention. She couldn't stop thinking about his hard body pressed up against hers. Or how he'd threatened to kiss her into being quiet. She shivered at the memory of his statement about tying her with drapery cords, but she wasn't too worried. He might have manhandled her. He might have partially undressed her without her permission or her noticing. But she didn't have so much as a bruise—except on her pride which still couldn't quite admit that she'd reacted to him on a primitive level that made her consider primping for dinner.

She wanted him. She ached to take a chance. Throw the dice and gamble.

Still, if she wanted to take Jason Parker up on his offer, her first priority had to be getting to know the man better. Dinner would be a fine starting place. And would commit her to absolutely nothing.

KIMBERLY WORE her favorite pair of jeans and an off-the-shoulder, black top to dinner. She never wore a bra with this particular top since the wide neck kept slipping to reveal one bared shoulder. And Kimberly didn't need a bra. One of the advantages of being small on top was that she had the option of wearing lingerie or not, without anyone else being the wiser.

Her only concession to seeing Jason at dinner was that she'd brushed her hair until it shone, then tied it back before applying a little powder, mascara and lip gloss. Pleased that she looked good, but still casual, she joined the other members of the tour group in the hotel dining room promptly at seven.

As if by design, Jason Parker entered the dining room at the exact same moment she did. He wore khaki slacks and a pinstriped navy-and-white shirt that did scrumptious things to set off his shoulders. His eyes found hers, his expression wary as if wondering what kind of mood he'd find her in.

But she no longer felt like throwing things at his head. Instead she wanted to know more about what was going on inside it. Until now she'd never thought to ask him why he'd agreed to Quinn's request—something she really needed to know. But that ques-

tion would have to be saved for a more private moment.

"Hi." She nodded politely, unwilling to let him know that she might be considering his offer.

"Good evening." Jason held out her chair for her and she took one of the last two seats at the round table set for nine. The room of polished woods and white linens could seat at least fifty people but the atmosphere was homey. The enticing scent of fresh baked scones and garlic butter made Kimberly's mouth water. Although she'd tried English tea she didn't like it as much as the full English breakfast of ham, eggs, sausages and more. Trying new foods intrigued her as much as did touring the quaint little waterfront towns and exploring the seaside.

Jason had already met Liam Short, their tour guide. Kimberly introduced him to two couples, the Jamisons: a history professor and his trophy wife, Trixie, from Phoenix, and the Barrs from Maine: a-down-to-earth couple on tour to celebrate their twentieth wedding anniversary. The other two singles were Alex Taylor, a certifiable surfer dude, and Caroline Morrison, a college coed who kept to herself and didn't speak often to anyone.

"We went to Eden today," Professor Jamison told them about the largest tourist attraction in southeastern England where huge domes displayed indoor greenhouses with plants from the Mediterranean, Africa and the tropics. "They have five domed areas, each climate-controlled with its own weather system."

"The flowers were beautiful." Trixie Jamison

checked her lipstick in a compact, then snapped it shut. She didn't quite interrupt her husband, but she seemed well aware that the professor would pontificate on his chosen subject if allowed to continue.

"We took a boat up the coast," volunteered Mr. Barr who'd told Kimberly that he was a third-generation fisherman. Mr. Barr had a weather-beaten face but kindly crinkles at the corners of brown eyes that he turned lovingly on his wife. His wife beamed at him through thick glasses and every so often, she patted her husband's hand.

As the group chattered about their day, Kimberly stole glances at Jason Parker.

Kimberly didn't say much. She preferred to listen and to watch and wonder if she could really make love with him. She found him attractive and charming when he wasn't holding her against a wall or pinned to a mattress. When she almost knocked over her glass of white wine, Jason's quick reflexes saved her from spilling more than a few drops. "Thanks."

"No problem."

"And how did your library research turn out, dear?" asked Mrs. Barr, who seemed interested in everyone and had a curiosity that had her asking their guide almost as many questions as Kimberly. Since Jason was new to their group, she added, "Kimberly is researching a script for Simitar Studios. We have a celebrity in our mix."

"I'm no celebrity," Kimberly told them. "I haven't even made my first sale yet."

"But you will," Professor Jamison said. "She has an in, since she works for the studio. And everyone

knows that the people in L.A. are a club that doesn't allow outsiders.''

Kimberly didn't bother to explain that she'd worked for an entire year before Quinn had consented even to read her work—and that was only because Maggie had nagged him into it. And she still wouldn't ever see her script made into a movie unless she wrote those love scenes.

''You sound as though you speak from experience,'' Jason commented.

''Oh, don't mind the professor,'' Trixie delicately touched her napkin to her lips, careful not to smudge her makeup. ''He reads everything. Four newspapers every morning. And dozens of magazines every month.''

Mrs. Barr buttered her dinner roll. ''Tell us about yourself, Mr. Parker—''

''Call me Jason.''

''Well, Jason, where do you hail from and what do you do for a living?''

Yes. Tell us, Jason Parker. Kimberly couldn't believe she knew so little about a man that she was considering going to bed with. Of course, she was no way close to making up her mind, but how could she not think about it after their outrageous conversation?

''I'm originally from Boston, but I haven't lived there in years. My work takes me all over the globe. I'm a movie consultant.''

The professor spoke between softly slurping spoonfuls of his shrimp bisque. ''What a coincidence that you both work in the movie business.''

"It's no coincidence at all," Jason answered easily. "I'm here to offer Kimberly technical assistance."

"Technical assistance?"

"My specialty is breaking and entering," Jason went on to speak with expertise about *The Heist*.

To Kimberly's ears, Jason sounded smooth and too charming, almost phony. But no one else at the table appeared the least bit suspicious, so she supposed her imagination was working overtime. Still, his lack of details nagged at her. She stopped tearing her garlic bread to shreds. "Where did you learn so much about the criminal world?"

"The military."

"In which branch did you serve?" Liam asked.

Before Jason could answer, a man rushed into the dining room. He whispered loudly to the maître d'. "I must speak to the mayor about urgent business."

The maître d' frowned and gestured for the stranger to lower his voice. The newcomer ignored the maître d' rushed past several groups of diners and didn't halt until he reached a table by the windows where two gentlemen stood to greet him.

"The *Book of Celts* is gone!"

A gray-haired gentleman wiped his mouth, then tossed the linen napkin down in disgust. "What do you mean the book is gone?"

"It was stolen right out of the library."

3

JASON WATCHED as Kimberly's eyes went as round as her butter dish and her skin paled as white as the linen tablecloth. When her bottom lip began to quiver, he watched in absolute fascination as she bit her lip and forced deep breaths of air into her lungs. He would have bet a jewel in his stash that she'd been just as surprised as he was to learn that the *Book of Celts* had been stolen—but she had had access to the book, she could have a partner he knew nothing about.

Unlikely. But possible.

Jason didn't believe in coincidences. And he didn't care how charming he found the quiver on Kimberly's lips or how much he might want to draw her into his arms and kiss the quiver away, he couldn't go with his gut reaction that she was an innocent—not when he'd caught her checking out that very same book while pretending to be someone else.

Earlier today after he'd let her go, she could have gone directly back to the library to steal the book, or after she'd cased the library and its security systems, she could have had an accomplice who'd done the dirty deed. She was good, all right.

Even as he whispered into her ear, ''We need to

talk, now,'' and they excused themselves from their dinner companions, he felt compelled to steady her as she tripped over a smooth spot on the carpet.

He kept a grip on her elbow as they strode past the other diners. Clearly distressed but determined to hold herself together, she didn't look to the right or the left. Her movements were still and he had the urge to pat her on the back, hold her close and tell her that she'd be fine.

After he'd caught her at the library, could she have gone through with her plans to steal the book? Was she so brazen that she figured her little miss innocent act would fool the local bobbies? And him?

Did she take him for a fool?

She exited the dining room with her head held high. He expected tears to flow the moment they were alone. He expected her to fling herself into his arms and ask him to keep quiet about what had happened that afternoon. Apparently he didn't know her well enough yet because she didn't do the expected.

Oh, no. She headed straight for the front desk, ignoring him completely.

He tightened his grip and slowed her down. ''Just where do you think you're going?''

''To call the police.''

He frowned at her, wondering for the second time that day if she was crazy. ''You're turning yourself in?''

''Of course not. I didn't *do* anything.'' She lifted her chin and her eyes flashed green fire at him. Another man might have been scorched, but Jason appreciated the heat.

Beneath that kind of heat a man would find passion. But he could never be that man if she did something so dumb as to turn herself in and get herself locked up in a cell.

He guided her toward a private corner of the empty reception area. "You used a fake ID and false pretenses to inspect the *Book of Celts*. And after we caught you, you had time to go back into the library to steal it."

"But I didn't." She snapped her spine as straight as a soldier at a court-martial. Those kissable lips drew tightly together and her beautiful eyes narrowed on him with an intensity that almost made him trust his instincts that she was innocent—almost but not quite. She failed to stare him down. "And since I have nothing to hide—"

"You're going to hand yourself over to the authorities like a Christmas goose ready to be cooked and carved?"

She folded her arms under her chest and speared him with a look of disdain. "I suppose you have a better idea?"

"Do nothing."

"But—"

"The police don't have a shred of evidence to tie you to the crime scene. Not even a fingerprint. You wore gloves, remember."

"But when you questioned me in the hallway that scene was caught on videotape. I admitted my real name, my nationality and who I work for." She raised a fist to her mouth and bit down on her knuckle, deep in thought. "I'm as good as caught."

"No. You aren't." He drew her hand from her mouth, rubbed the spot she'd bitten and guided her onto a sofa in a comfy nook next to a marble fireplace and far enough away from the reception desk to give them privacy. "After I let you go, I returned to the security office. That guard deserves to be fired because he didn't see our conversation in the hallway as he was off on a tea break. And I erased the tape."

"Why?"

He could hardly tell her that he was a man wanted on three continents by authorities who were looking into the disappearance of stolen jewelry and then expect to work himself into her good graces. He couldn't tell her that he habitually avoided having his picture taken. Allowing his face to be seen on a videotape was anathema to a man in his profession. He couldn't even tell her that he'd given her a fake name.

He'd erased the tape to hide *his* presence, not hers. But now he needed to give her a believable answer. Whether a guilty spy or an innocent woman, Kimberly seemed to have a bright mind, but if she were truly a spy, he had to come up with a good answer. Many times in his career, he would have been caught if his brain hadn't worked just as fast as his fingers.

He lowered his voice. "It pays to be careful, and I have an image to uphold."

"What are you saying?"

"If the guard had decided to sell that tape, my standing in certain circles could be compromised."

"Huh?"

"Haven't you seen those tapes of people making love in elevators and closets and hallways that have

shown up on television and the Internet? I did unbutton your shirt, remember?''

"So what?"

"They might have thought we were having kinky sex—'' not that he would have turned her down ''—and sold the tape to the highest bidder.''

"Are you married?"

"Hardly," he replied thinking that an odd question for her to ask at a moment like this one.

"Why would a single man care about a video-tape?"

"We aren't all from Hollywood where a sex scandal will enhance our image. My conservative parents wouldn't like it."

"Oh, right. You stole a tape so a picture of you unbuttoning my blouse wouldn't show up on the Internet?"

He pretended not to hear her sarcasm. "It's okay. The tape is no more."

Maybe she'd feel grateful enough to tell him the truth, but she still looked suspicious.

"And the guard just let you waltz into his office, use his equipment and erase the tape?"

"He had to answer a call of nature." Jason had just saved her cute little ass, but she was scowling at him. "What?"

"I don't know whether to thank you or thwap you upside the head for telling me such a ridiculous story."

"I wouldn't object to a kiss of appreciation."

"Has anyone ever told you that you have a one-track mind?"

He leaned close to her, knee touching knee. Their lips were less than an inch apart and he could smell the scent of wine on her breath. "One-track? I see nothing wrong with holding to a course of action as long as that track takes us where we want to go."

"We? This might sound strange to you, but there is no we. I don't kiss men who I don't know a thing about."

She might have protested, but she didn't pull away. And she didn't seem to be considering talking to the local authorities any longer, thank goodness. He supposed he should be satisfied with the progress he'd made on the case, but concentrating was hard when all he wanted to do was carry her up to his room, undress her slowly and make love to her on his crisp clean sheets.

She was sitting close enough for a lock of her hair to brush against his arm. She was talking to him, not shouting. And she now owed him big-time. He could take his time deciding when to collect.

He tried to sound patient. "What do you want to know?"

"Why did you accept Quinn's offer?"

"You don't want to know."

No man would easily volunteer the answer to a question like that. She was going to have to work to draw this answer out of him—even if it was a lie. He couldn't exactly tell her he'd accepted the mission for the Shey Group due to a promise he'd made Kincaid that kept him out of jail.

"I wouldn't have asked if I didn't want to know."

"You'll think badly of me."

"I'll think worse of you if you don't give me an answer," she countered.

"Quinn faxed me your picture."

"I'm no actress with head shots in Quinn's file cabinet. Where did he get my picture?"

"I have no idea, but a man like Quinn has resources. If he wanted your picture taken, any photographer with a telephoto lens could snap a photo from a block away and you'd never know."

"So you saw my picture," she prodded.

"And I agreed."

She raised a brow that voiced her skepticism. "Quinn sent you my picture and you agreed? You haven't told me why."

"Because I liked the picture he sent. I was immediately attracted to you."

He figured she would ask what about her attracted him. Women loved compliments, even the experienced ones who filled his normal hunting grounds. But she had to be difficult.

"Can I see the picture?" she asked sweetly, but her eyes had narrowed to those sexy slits that meant she was all riled up again.

"It's in my room. We could go there and I'll show you mine if you show me yours."

"I'm not going to your room."

He tried to look disappointed while making a mental note to find a picture of her—tonight. She was one smart, sexy lady. To stay ahead of her, he had to anticipate her next move.

KIMBERLY FELT as though strange forces were sucking her into a vortex. She needed time to think and get her feet back under her. She wanted to go over every word Jason Parker had said to her because she didn't believe him. Despite all his help, despite his charm, something didn't ring true, but she couldn't put her finger on it.

Had Maggie, with Quinn's help, handpicked this man to be her lover?

Every time she just thought about writing those love scenes she knocked something over, tripped or gasped for air. Maybe it was because she wanted so desperately to do them right. However, thinking about researching those scenes with Jason Parker was enough to give her heart palpitations.

She didn't like the way she wanted to trust him. She knew all too well from her parents' example that people were often not who they seemed. Their friends and neighbors had all believed her folks were civil servants. No one suspected they secretly worked as undercover agents for the CIA.

Kimberly had kept their secret for years and she wasn't accustomed to opening up to anyone. Then again, she'd never been alone in a foreign country dealing with acts of an illegal nature. Although she hadn't stolen that book, she knew how suspicious her actions today would look to the authorities. And she wasn't naive enough to believe that innocent people never got locked up, especially if they were foreigners.

She was about to rise to her feet, tell Jason goodnight and head to her room, when two English policemen entered the hotel's foyer. The bobbies headed

to the desk, had a short conversation then headed straight toward Jason and her.

Damn.

Maybe Jason hadn't erased the tape. Or maybe someone else had seen through her disguise.

Beside her Jason rose to her feet. "Good evening. Something we can do for you, gentlemen?"

"Your name, sir?"

"Jason Parker."

"You were at the library this afternoon?"

"Yes." Jason's voice was as smooth as maple syrup, but the policemen weren't looking at him. "Madam, are you Kimberly Hayward?"

"Yes."

"Did you visit the library this afternoon?"

"I did." She saw no point in denying it. Several members of her group had seen her there. But had they seen Dr. Johnson? More importantly, did they know that Kimberly Hayward and Dr. Johnson were the same person?

"Did either of you see a brunette woman wearing a navy business suit, white blouse and glasses?"

"I saw the woman in question on a security monitor and went down to talk to her, but she'd fled before I got there," Jason lied.

But what would happen when the cops interviewed the library guard and learned that Jason's story didn't jibe with the guard's? She supposed it was Jason's word against the other man's.

"Could you identify her?" the officer asked Jason.

"Maybe. Maybe not. The picture was fuzzy."

"What about you, ma'am? Did you see her?"

Not unless she'd looked in the mirror, she hadn't. Kimberly didn't trust herself to speak. She just shook her head and the two police officers thanked them and entered the dining area.

Barely daring to believe she'd gotten away with it, she couldn't move, but somehow Jason was cradling her against his chest, murmuring into her ear as if she needed steadying. "You did fine. They're looking for a brunette. Just hold it together for a few more minutes."

It would take more than a few questions from the bobbies for her to fall into pieces. However, she welcomed his using the occasion to draw her into his arms. She snuggled tighter and clasped her arms around him.

His shirt smelled clean, but masculine. His arms around her felt like bands of protection. Resting her head against his chest and listening to the regular thump of his heart had a stimulating effect on her excited nerves.

It seemed the most natural thing in the world to tip up her head and offer her lips. He didn't hesitate. He took his time, first brushing his mouth lightly over hers, then nibbling and nipping before finally molding his lips to hers.

His mouth was warm and demanding, his breath fresh. But most of all, his kiss reminded her of banked embers before they burst into flames. Somehow, her fingers threaded through his thick dark hair. Her chest pressed against his and her nipples immediately hardened.

Their tongues mingled and she drew him in like a

rich, frothy dessert that sharpened the senses and spiked her hunger. His hair beneath her fingertips was silky soft and thick. Tension arched her back and their hips pressed together until she could feel his erection pulsing hard and urgent.

She should pull back. She needed to think, to assess, to reconcile her aroused senses with everything that had happened today. Her close call with the bobbies had her edgy enough to believe kissing him wasn't such a big risk, that making love would be a desirable conclusion to an exciting day.

But did fantasizing about making love with him make the reality more reasonable sounding? She should break this kiss.

Instead, she hooked one foot around his ankle, demanding more. The warmth of his hand on her bare shoulder felt so good she wished he'd keep going. But he drew tiny circles of heat, which shot right to her core.

"Excuse me. Madam. Is this man accosting you again?"

Huh? Reluctantly, Kimberly broke their kiss to face the grinning tour guide Liam Short, surrounded by the rest of the tour group.

"I believe the lady was enjoying herself," Jason told Liam. Then he turned to her. "Well?"

"Uh. Ah." Her spinning thoughts wouldn't settle. "I'm sorry. What was the question?"

"You want me to call the bobbies back—"

"No."

Kimberly realized that her answer had been too sharp. Liam had only been teasing her about kissing

Jason. What the hell was wrong with her? She had to settle down. She shouldn't have kissed Jason at all, but she hadn't been thinking right since the moment she'd met him.

At the thought of the entire tour group having just witnessed their kiss, she sighed. If they hadn't been interrupted, they might still be locking lips. Oh my, could he kiss. Her legs still felt weak as clotted cream and she knocked right into a table. A lamp wobbled. A glass vase teetered and would have toppled except for Jason's quick save and steadying hand.

The man had quick reflexes. He seemed to do everything well—from erasing a tape that kept her out of jail to kissing her until she could barely think straight. And now every cell in her body seemed attracted to him. It took every ounce of will not to step back into his arms.

Sheesh. Practical Kimberly never felt giddy about men. Not even movie stars. So what was happening here?

"My dear," the professor pontificated, "there's no need for embarrassment. Greek poets described a kiss as the key to paradise and claimed one kiss could unlock the heart's most secret desires."

Liam chuckled. "Our Celtic ancestors believed a kiss had magical powers. The breath from a kiss was believed to contain the essence of life and when lovers caressed it brought about the mingling of souls."

"Oh, what a lovely sentiment. Just lovely," the professor's wife said.

As if not to be outdone by their guide, the professor

continued, "Throughout history the kiss has been a timeless act of love—"

Love? More like lust, Kimberly thought, but kept the notion to herself. Lust that might very well carry her through those love scenes. However, she'd already drawn enough unwanted attention to herself, thank you very much.

"—and devotion. It's been said that one heartfelt kiss is equal to a thousand words."

"Cool, dude," Alex signaled a thumbs-up and walked away.

But Caroline, the college student who rarely said a word, started to speak, and not to anyone in particular. "A study in polarity."

"Excuse me?" Jason asked.

Caroline glanced out the window at the stars, as if consulting her muse. "Standing 180 degrees apart. You two exert a tremendous pull on one another."

"My dear," Mrs. Barr spoke up in her thick Maine accent. "I didn't know you were into astrology."

Astrology? Were all the kooks coming out tonight? Kimberly shared a long look with Jason and when he rolled his blue eyes toward the ceiling, she bit back a grin.

"She's clearly an Aquarius and he the proud Leo, don't you think?" Caroline's question required no answer. "Their relationship will have a magnetic attraction, irresistible in its charm, but they must overcome extreme differences in attitude and lifestyle."

"It's been wonderful meeting you all. Good evening." Jason took Kimberly's arm and escorted her away from the others.

"I *am* an Aquarius." Kimberly muttered.

"So she caught a glimpse of your passport." Jason's mocking tone revealed that he clearly didn't believe in astrology.

"So are you a Leo?"

"She had a one in twelve chance of guessing correctly. Not bad odds—"

"If you're a gambler."

Kimberly stopped at the stairway landing, unwilling to go up those stairs with Jason after the sizzling kiss they'd shared. Her reaction to that kiss had been so unexpected, so primitive and wonderfully hot that she had trouble believing that it had happened. But it had.

She'd once done research for a script about lips and learned that different-shaped lips revealed character traits. She hadn't put much store by the descriptions but she and Cate had talked about the subject. Supposedly generous lips revealed a fun-loving, broadminded and generous person. Curvaceous lips meant one had a passionate nature. Rosebud lips belonged to those with a reserved and sensitive personality. Pouting lips gave the impression of raw sensuality.

When she found herself staring at Jason's slender-shaped lips and recalling that his belonged to those with secretly sensual personalities, she heated up all over again. All that talk about kissing, followed by the most sensual kiss she'd ever shared, had her off-kilter.

"Do I have something between my teeth, or are you staring at my mouth because you want me to kiss you again?" Jason asked her with that half grin of

amusement that was too sexy for a man with his instincts for moving in on a woman when she was vulnerable.

No way was she answering his question—not even to herself. "Are you deliberately trying to make me uncomfortable?"

"I'm trying to make you aware that you want me."

"I didn't exactly protest when you kissed me. I'm not shaking. I'm not scared of you."

"Of course, you aren't. You're afraid of yourself."

"What?"

"Of your reaction to me. You want me. You want to research those erotic scenes with me, but you won't admit it."

"Really." She wished she could have put more conviction into her statement, but the man had her so flabbergasted that she didn't know how to respond. No one had ever challenged her the way Jason did. But then she'd never given anyone else the chance.

"Your eyes give you away. Those exotic, tilted green eyes that say sweep me off my feet."

"Yeah, right." She tried to sound angry but couldn't inject enough heat into her voice, not with the way his tone had massaged her into a slow burn of desire.

"You can't stop watching my mouth." He spoke softly, enthusiastically, convincingly. "Your pulse is faster than normal. Your eyes are dilated."

Her heart beat a melody against her ribs. "I think that's enough."

"Your nipples are all excited to see me, darling." He edged closer.

She retreated a step until her bottom backed into a wall. "I'm nobody's darling, and I didn't need to hear that."

"You didn't *want* to hear that. Are you the kind of woman that ignores the simmering tension building in her?"

How did the smooth operator know what she was feeling? He couldn't see her churning emotions. Nor could he know of the damp heat between her thighs. "I don't do one-night stands."

"Oh, darling. I intend to share much more than one night with you. In fact, the screenplay calls for several love scenes, doesn't it?"

While she'd written the screenplay, she'd hadn't yet decided how to add the love scenes. "I haven't agreed to—"

"But you want to."

"Would you please stop telling me what I want."

"Okay."

He had to be the most frustrating man she'd ever met. How could she argue with him when he'd just agreed with her? How could she push him away when every word he'd spoken was true? She wanted to drag him up to her bed, rip off his clothes and make mad passionate love. Not because Maggie had challenged her to check out the love scenes she wrote. Not because making love would further her career. But because she was in lust. She'd never in her life wanted to act so irresponsibly. And she had no idea why she did now.

She'd never been so close to throwing away every

hesitation and belief she'd held, turning off her brain and just indulging in mind-blowing sex. If Maggie were here right now, her friend would tell her to go for him. To just do it.

4

"GOOD NIGHT." Kimberly retreated up the steps before she changed her mind about inviting Jason to join her.

Coward!

No, sensible, Kimberly argued with herself.

Kimberly wasn't Maggie. She didn't have her friend's courage. And besides, when Maggie had finally made her move on her boss, literally masquerading as a movie star and seducing the man, she'd known Quinn for years. Whereas, Kimberly had just met Jason today.

She needed time to think, and she couldn't hop into bed with a stranger just because she felt like it—and still respect herself or her decision.

Which didn't mean she had to suffer. Kimberly was a big girl. And in the new millennium, no single woman required a man to solve sexual frustration vexations. Knowing she could accomplish two goals at once, since it was time she tried out one of the scenarios in her script, she hurried to her room. She envisioned a hot bubble bath, soft music, candles and a humongous orgasm to take off the edge. Afterwards, with her body relaxed, she'd be able to think about Jason's offer.

Kimberly locked the door to her room and headed straight to the oversized tub in the marble bathroom. She ran hot water into the tub, poured in a handful of bubble bath and then shed her clothes while she turned on her CD player and searched for candles. Within minutes, she'd settled into the half-filled tub, leaned back her head onto a plump, folded towel and closed her eyes, letting the steaming heat soak into her tight muscles as the tub kept filling.

Images of Jason Parker immediately inundated her. Those piercing blue eyes. His sensual lips perpetually quirked in amusement—usually at something she'd just done or said. Man oh man, did the guy have a set of shoulders. And that magical kiss had been indescribably delicious.

Using a soapy loofa, Kimberly skimmed it over her shoulders and breasts. As she recalled how Jason had noticed her body's response to him, her face heated once again. She couldn't figure the man out, since he seemed one giant mass of contradictions. He spoke like an educated man, but he didn't follow the rules of accepted behavior. He'd backed her against that wall in the library like a pirate. He'd barged into her room like a Viking conqueror. And, when the police arrived, he'd assessed and evaluated her options with the cool logic of a trial attorney.

Who was Jason Parker?

He wanted her to believe that he'd stepped into Quinn's plans because he'd been attracted to her photograph. Well, Kimberly was no movie legend like Laine Lamonde and she didn't buy his story. But was she overly suspicious? Did the fact that her parents

had led secret lives color the way she viewed the world? Yet, everything he'd told her made perfect sense, right down to his knowledge about what was in the script.

The soft sensual voice of Enya, combined with the scent of jasmine candles had eased back the immediacy of her trying day. She stroked the loofa pad along the sensitive flesh of her upper thighs, parting her legs in anticipation of satisfying her body's craving to be touched, petted and pampered, a craving that Jason had begun with one kiss and that she would finish alone—but happily contented. Finally her jangled nerves had almost settled in favor of a blossoming sexual tension.

Her door creaked.

Someone had entered her room without knocking, without her permission. She should have been scared, but she knew only one person in all of England who would have the audacity...and exasperation rose up her throat.

She stared through the open bathroom door, hoping she'd been mistaken. Perhaps the disturbing noise hadn't been a creaking floor but just water going through the pipes.

She called out. "Who's there?"

"Jason."

She hadn't been mistaken. And her irritation revved to anger.

"Get out."

"And good evening to you, too."

She didn't want to see him. Didn't want him to see her. She was naked, damn it. How the man always

seemed to catch her when she was most vulnerable, she had no idea—but he had to stop.

Why hadn't she shoved a chair under her doorknob? She'd known he could and would pick her lock. But his gentlemanly air kept fooling her, because he was no gentleman.

And now she was undressed, with only bubbles up to her neck and a loofa pad to hide her bare skin. To reach the towel hanging on the rack, she'd have to stand up and expose herself.

"Damn it. Jason, you can't just come in my room whenever you please."

"Sure I can. And keep your voice down." His voice carried to her clearly from the bedroom. She heard drawers opening and closing, then the hangers in her closet, squeaking as he shoved the hangers back and forth on the rod. She heard a zipper opening and realized he'd found the duffel bag with all the costumes she'd packed to match the roles she needed to play in the script.

What was he doing? Fumbling through her lacy underwear? And how dare he sneak into her room and then tell her to keep her voice down.

She had to make a play for her towel. Gathering her feet under her, talking more to get an idea where he actually was than because she wanted an answer, she pulled herself to her knees. "What are you doing here?"

She shoved to her feet and water and bubble bath trickled down her bare skin in noisy rivulets.

"Making sure you—" He poked his head through

the door and caught her standing there, totally exposed and backlit by candlelight.

She crossed her hands over her breasts. "Oh, God. Go away."

"Not a chance, gorgeous."

"Turn your back," she demanded.

"Turn my back on the most stunning sight I've seen in a week? I don't think so."

"Damn you to hell."

"Honey, I think I've just gone to heaven. You're amazingly hot." His hand closed over the towel one second before hers did and he snapped it out of her reach.

She wanted to scream in frustration. But the thought of calling for help and having her entire tour group find her standing in her tub without any clothes made her stifle her first instinct. Instead she lowered herself and slid back under the bubbles.

It took only a moment to realize he had her trapped. Naked. Alone.

Outraged enough to do something drastic—yet too surprised to do more than sputter, she supposed another woman might have been screaming about now. But the banked lust in his eyes, the amused quirk of his mouth and the way he leaned so still against the doorway told her he had himself under control.

Nix that. He had most of himself under control. In the flickering candlelight she could make out a very definite bulge in his slacks.

His tone was dark, husky and shot a shiver of lust straight to her core. "Of course. I want you."

He'd caught her looking at his crotch. And so many

emotions warred for supremacy—embarrassment, anger, lust and surprise—that she just froze.

He removed his jacket and hung it on the back of the doorknob. Then he leaned closer, his eyes dark. "It's okay to say you want me, too."

Finally, she found her voice again, but it didn't carry the conviction she'd aimed for. "You can't stay here."

"Of course I can." He slipped off his shoes. "Liam told me the cops are searching the hotel room by room."

"And you came here because?" she prodded, her heart dancing up her throat as he unbuttoned his shirt. Why was he taking off his shirt in her bathroom? She could think of only one reason, he aimed to join her in the tub, and she didn't like the idea one bit.

"It occurred to me that you might not have hidden the evidence."

"Evidence?" He was confusing her. Having this calm discussion while he was taking off his clothes and she was hiding under bubbles, meant she had trouble keeping track of the conversation. "I told you I didn't take the book."

"I'm talking about your clothes." He removed his shirt and hung it nearly over his jacket. His chest matched his shoulders. Broad and muscular and dusted with a triangle of dark hair that disappeared beneath the waistband of his slacks.

"I don't have on any clothes."

He chuckled. "Yes, I can see that." He unzipped his pants. "But I'm talking about the navy suit Dr.

Johnson wore. And the wig. It wouldn't look good if the police found these items in your room.''

With a careless toss, Jason flicked her navy skirt, jacket and wig into the tub. Then he stepped out of his slacks, neatly folded them so the creases matched up and hung them over the towel rack. Her mouth went dry—whether in fear of the cops finding the wig and navy suit in the tub or of his muscular physique, she didn't know. Her heart was pounding hard, but no blood seemed to be going to her brain.

She looked from the suit and wig floating in the bubbles to him. ''Look. If you think for one damn minute that you're getting into this tub and that I'll—''

''Hush.'' He flicked off his boxers and sank into the tub, making room for himself between her legs.

At the same moment, there was a loud knock on the door. Two police officers identified themselves and pounded harder on her door.

''What do we do?'' she whispered, wishing she'd never come to England, or written a script, or met the man sharing her bath with such amusement in his eyes.

Jason settled back, his long legs reaching to her bare hips. He called out to the policemen. ''It's unlocked. Come on in and join the party.''

''Are you crazy?'' she whispered, tugging the shirt, jacket and wig under the bubbles.

He dunked his hands under the water and gripped her ankles. ''Don't be shy darling. We have nothing to hide. These gentleman can't see anything below

these bubbles and I doubt they'll want to interrupt our bath any more than necessary.''

''Of course not, sir.''

''What can we do for you?'' Jason asked, his palms sliding suggestively up and down the arches of her feet.

''Can we have permission to search the room?''

''Yes,'' Jason told them.

''No!'' she objected.

Jason chuckled. ''The lady's a little shy.'' His fingers were working their way up her feet to her toes. He knew just which muscles to knead but now was no time to be playing footsie or to be giving a massage.

''We won't be long, sir.''

''Take your time.'' Jason chuckled knowingly at her predicament. If she protested his presence in the bath, screamed for help, the cops would find the suit and wig. ''The water's hot and the view is wonderful.''

Oh God. She'd scooted back, trying to avoid his hold on her feet and her breasts had come out of the water. She sank back down, right where he wanted her, wondering how in hell she'd gotten herself into such a mess. His gaze glued to her face, his fingers tickled her arches, teased between her toes and taunted their way up her ankles.

He leaned his head close to hers, but allowed his voice to carry. ''Shh. Trust me. I'm taking care of things.''

But she didn't trust him. He seemed too good at

averting problems with the cops. And once again she wondered if he was the man he seemed.

Kimberly realized the cops probably thought that he was making love to her and he was talking about using a condom. However, he obviously meant that he didn't expect the police to find the navy suit and wig and after they searched, their suspicion of her would be over.

But she couldn't spare too many thoughts for the police, not with his roving hands on her body. He knew just where to touch her and how much pressure to apply. Her feet tingled, and as she realized that she was sitting there naked with no way to stop his roving hands from going all the way up her legs—short of calling the police into the bathroom, she shivered with all kinds of desperate thoughts racing through her.

Again, he didn't bother keeping down his voice. "Don't move, darling, or I'll tell them everything we're doing."

The cops in the other room chuckled. No doubt they thought Jason was threatening to tell them about lovemaking. But she knew he was talking about the suit and wig.

She clenched her fists, wondering if she should just confess to the cops. That's when he shifted position slightly. Water rippled over her breasts and between her legs, making her so much more aware of her nudity. And where his roaming hands could so easily travel next.

She sucked in a gasp and clenched her fingers.

"That's right. Keep your hands on the edge of the

tub, darling. And look at me. I want to watch your eyes while I rub your—''

''Keep your voice down.''

''Now darling. Those officers can't see us.'' He raised his voice, his thumb finding a knot in the arch of her foot. ''Can you men see the lady?''

''No, sir.''

Her face flamed with heat from the combination of what he was doing to her and what he made it sound like he was doing to her. She could only imagine what those police officers must have been thinking about Americans. At least they wouldn't be that surprised when they found the bag with racy lingerie inside. But she had no idea what they would think of…Jason's fingers soothed out another aching nerve and she bit back a gasp. She hadn't known her feet could be this sensitive.

His thumb kept flicking up and down over her arch. When he reached the ball of her foot and worked between the joints of her toes, she closed her eyes and bit back a moan.

''Look at me, darling. There's no escaping my plans for you.''

She opened her eyes and let him see the pleasure swimming there. And his fingers kept playing, slowly, languidly, stroking first one foot, then the other, slowly, seductively. She couldn't say exactly when the policemen left, was never sure, when she just gave herself up to the heaven of Jason's foot massage.

He possessed skilled hands, and every atom of her skin now craved that he give the rest of her the same treatment as he'd given her feet. She wanted to press

herself against him like a cat in need of petting. And his hands on her ankles never stopped their slow, smooth stroking, seducing her with a sudden wild and wanton willingness to let him touch wherever he pleased.

"Stand up and let me rinse the soap off you," he requested.

At that point her feet tingled so wonderfully she didn't want to put weight on them. And she was so mellow that she felt no embarrassment about standing naked in front of him. If he wanted to look, let him.

He pulled the plug from the drain and turned on the shower. Then he helped her to her feet and she leaned against him under the cascade of warm water. He lifted her lips to share another kiss. Would this kiss be as magical as the first?

It was better. Pressed flesh to flesh with the water cascading over them, his mouth found hers. And his hands that never stopped moving stroked her back, his fingers threading through her hair. She leaned into him and he gathered her closer, giving and taking, seducing and ravishing, tempting and luring her into a state of bliss that made thinking inconsequential and unnecessary.

When he finally pulled back, his eyes dark with passion, she had to grab his arm to steady herself. His kiss wasn't just a kiss. His caresses weren't just caresses. Somehow he'd intoxicated her with his male essence and she could easily become addicted to the kind of pleasure he dished out.

When he'd dried her with the bath towel, she'd had no more doubts about wanting to make love to a man

she'd only just met. Her body and mind had finally gotten together and set their priorities straight.

She wanted Jason in her bed. She wanted him to make wild and crazy love to her.

When he reached for his clothes, she figured that she could simply have a good time taking them back off. But when she looked at him, he was all business. She bit her bottom lip. He had her all turned on. His erection under his pants was blatant. So why weren't they rolling across her mattress?

"Aren't we going to—"

"Not yet."

"We aren't?" Disappointment shot through her. Didn't he know how hard it had been for her to get past the fact that they'd just met? Didn't he understand her inhibitions were down after sharing the bath with him and that her body was ready to make love? Plus, she had herself all convinced that she wanted to make love to him—even if he was a stranger. How could he let all that wonderful buildup fizzle into nothing? She wanted to stamp her foot in frustration. Or better yet, tackle him on the bed.

"First, we're going out."

"Why?"

"Disappointed, are you?" He buttoned his shirt and tucked the tail into his slacks. Finally he slipped into his jacket. "You coming with me or not?"

He didn't want to make love to her. Naturally, the first thing she did was wonder what she'd done wrong. Had she been too passive? Too slow to make up her mind? Or had he just not found her sexy enough?

None of the above. She'd seen his erection. Kimberly might be confused, but her feminine instincts hadn't abandoned her. If he wanted her to put on her clothes so they could go out—well then fine. However, after that foot massage, he was going to get back a little of his own teasing.

Kimberly headed straight to the costume bag and pulled out the sexiest lingerie she could find. The dark green bra, all lacy and see-through, cupped her breasts, almost but not quite, creating cleavage, but didn't even cover her nipples. Next, she shimmied into panties, a garter belt and silky black stockings that she took her time drawing over her feet, calves and thighs. She turned to face him with a sexy grin. "You sure you want me to finish dressing?"

"Ah, darling. I knew from the moment I set eyes on you that we were going to have such fun together."

"Fine." She donned the shortest micromini skirt she owned, boots and pulled a jean jacket right over her bra—no blouse. That would give Mr. We-need-to-go-out something to think about.

"You're only going to secure one button?"

She bit back a grin. "If it comes unfastened, I'm sure you'll let me know."

He gestured toward the door. "The sooner we leave, the sooner we can get back. But in the meantime we're both going to have some fun. You're never going to know when I'm going to slip my fingers under your jacket, perhaps tweak a nipple."

"Of course, I'll know." Her nipples responded to his words as if he'd touched her. And she realized

too late that her lack of a blouse wasn't going to tease just him. She, too, would suffer from the effect of her hardened nipples rubbing against her jacket. But she wasn't about to change her mind, not when she felt daring—and glad of it.

It was his turn to chuckle. "I'll look forward to the challenge."

She realized she'd just given him permission to slip his hand under her jacket. Instead of alarm, she was anticipating his move. "Why can't we stay here and—"

"Because we need to get rid of the suit and wig." He strode into the bathroom and she could hear him wringing water out of the clothing and wig. "I'm not taking any chances with your safety. I'm hoping that allowing the police to search your room dismissed any suspicions they might have had of you."

"That's why you invited them in?"

"Most innocent people would have done so."

She raised a brow. "That's not what I asked."

"And I couldn't resist the opportunity to climb into that tub with you."

"Somehow I believe that for once you're being truthful."

"But if the police are still suspicious and watching us, once my hand goes under your jacket, they'll just think we're playing kinky games."

"But—"

He lightly squeezed her hand. "Trust me, darling. No man in his right mind is going to be thinking about the evidence down my sleeve, not when my hand's up your blouse."

She'd been thinking about making love and all he seemed to care about was the police and her suit and her wig. "Surely there have to be others to—"

His mouth closed over hers in a hard, demanding kiss that left no room for her to breathe, no chance for her to protest. He held her so close her breasts pressed against him and her nipples tightened into nubs so hard she thought she might climax from his kiss alone.

She barely resisted straddling one of his hard thighs and rubbing against him to ease the building ache. And when he ended the kiss much too soon with a soft chuckle, spun her around and marched her toward the door, she didn't want to let him know how badly she was trembling—so she simply walked through the door he held open for her.

"We're going out. And when we get back, I'm going to give you the best lovemaking you've ever had."

"Promises. Promises." She ought to give him back some smart retort. But she hadn't expected his kiss to leave her all weak and warm inside. He'd been touching and kissing her all evening.

Never before had she let a man put moves on her so fast. That foot massage had been one of the sexiest experiences of her life. Sitting naked in that tub with him was the kind of act she could envision for a script—but not for herself. She was practical, down-to-earth Kimberly. She didn't do passion. She didn't ever forget that strangers could have all kinds of secrets or that she wanted to know those secrets before she considered making love to a man.

However, all her commonsense seemed to just soar out the window when it came to Jason Parker. He overwhelmed her in ways she wasn't equipped to combat.

Her body was wound up tighter than a sprinter waiting for the starter's pistol. Not only hadn't he made love to her, he hadn't let her work off any of the sexual tension in her bath. Instead, he'd upped the heat another few degrees.

She'd never felt this on edge in her life. She needed some distance. He was so close, she could smell his masculine scent and tried to take a step or two away.

When his fingers slipped up her thigh and snapped her garter, she almost jumped out of her skin in surprise.

"Ow."

"Be good and stay close."

"I don't want to be good. Nor do I want to wait for you to decide—"

She stopped talking at the sight of the crowd in the hotel foyer. Men and women from their tour group were staring up at them.

5

"DID WE MISS something?" Jason asked smoothly. He'd escaped from so many tight scrapes he'd lost count, especially since he almost always talked his way out of a rough spot—a knack he'd honed to serve him well over the years.

Beside him, Kimberly was as tense as a cornered fox. He'd hoped snapping her garter would take her mind off the crowd waiting for them at the bottom of the stairs and cause her to relax, but that hadn't seemed to work. Although he couldn't account for every minute of her time after she left the library, he believed her an innocent bystander, under suspicion by her government for reasons he had yet to clear up. A professional spy would have much more self-control, better excuses and an impeccable cover.

Unless she was a professional pretending to throw them all off with her innocence.

The circular logic could have made his head ache if he let it. Instead of worrying over her guilt or innocence, he simply enjoyed the sight of her long, toned legs, barely covered by that short, short skirt as she walked in front of him. And he enjoyed the sight even more for already having seen what her clothes were now keeping hidden.

The memory of her exquisite breasts and coral-

tipped nipples framed in green lace made him grateful for his loose slacks. Kimberly possessed a perfectly proportioned body, slender shoulders, a tiny waist and trim hips. And gorgeous slanted green eyes that widened with wonder, then snapped closed when she kissed him. And, oh-hot-damn, had she melted against him during that kiss.

In contrast, she now stood as tense and rigid as a barber pole, almost as if she expected the police to produce the stolen book and accuse her of the theft. However, if she *had* lifted it, she hadn't stashed the relic in her room. His search might have been quick, but he'd been thorough, and the police had searched, too, and found nothing.

"The authorities still haven't found the *Book of Celts*," Liam told them as they reached the last step and joined the rest of the tour group. "But the bobbies are requesting we delay our departure for another twenty-four hours."

A babble of voices rose up in argument. The professor's was loudest. "That would limit our time in Scotland. I insist we stick to our schedule. They have no evidence to make us stay."

"The police can't stop us from leaving, can they?" Mrs. Barr asked their guide.

"No, Madam. The choice is ours."

"We should blow this town," Alex agreed as he sneaked a look at Kimberly's legs.

As much as Jason didn't blame the kid for looking, he nevertheless didn't like the idea of him ogling her. Jason found nothing odd about his possessive behavior; he didn't believe in sharing. Besides, he'd move

on soon enough. But while they were together, he wanted exclusivity.

Mr. Barr slung an arm over his wife's shoulder. "They've already searched all of our rooms, and we've cooperated fully. I see no reason to postpone our plans."

"Then we're agreed?" Liam asked.

Beside Jason, Kimberly didn't say a word. Was she avoiding calling attention to herself? Or was the group simply mirroring her opinion so she needn't say anything? Possibly, she just didn't care one way or the other. But since her script was so important to her, she obviously had a scheduled agenda and other places to check out during her trip. Seemed to him, if she was on the up and up, she wouldn't mind speaking up against a delay.

Wishing he had hard evidence to back up his instinctive belief of her innocence, he walked out of the hotel holding her hand, the silence between them comfortable. Her heels clicked pleasantly on the cobblestone street, but would make it easy for anyone to follow them. Appearing innocent as the summer breeze had advantages. To any interested onlooker, he and Kimberly would appear to be friends or lovers out for a late-night stroll—not allies on a secret mission.

The deep shadows cast by steep-pitched cottages lent a romantic aura to their journey. So did the half moon that shone brightly enough to light their way down to the wharf.

"Where are we going?" she asked.

"How do you feel about boats?"

"I'm not especially passionate about them. Why?"

"Oh, come on, where's your adventurous spirit? How about a kayak ride at midnight?"

"You want me to paddle a boat?" Her voice raised in exasperation. Then she leaned her head to his and whispered. "Can't we just throw the stuff off a bridge?"

"Someone might see us," he whispered back.

She stopped right in the middle of the street and tugged on his arm. "How far out are we paddling this kayak?"

Obviously, she'd taken to heart his warning about being seen. "Let me worry over the details."

"That's the problem."

"What?"

"You don't look worried."

He chuckled, took her arm and started strolling again. "Don't you know how to swim?"

"Not well enough to cross the English Channel."

"That won't be necessary. We'll be in a—"

"Kayak?" She shivered. "The only kind of boat I want to take is one that requires reservations, like the Queen Mary."

"She's retired."

"That's just a detail."

"It's the details that can trip you up." He drew her under his arm and tugged her against his side. He spoke in a low whisper. "Be very careful what you say."

"Why?" She started to turn her head.

"Don't look."

"But—"

"Someone's following us."

"Oh, God." She walked faster.

He slowed her back down. "Easy. We don't want them to know that we know."

"Why?"

"Because we want to look innocent."

"We *are* innocent."

He dragged her to a stop. "I think it's time you kissed me again."

Despite his earlier warning not to look for their pursuer, she glanced over her shoulder to check the road behind them. "You want me to stop right here and kiss you?"

"Yes." He slid both hands under her jacket, enjoying the warmth of her flesh, liking the way she shivered and shimmied at his touch. He recalled that sexy bra that left her nipples exposed to his touch and let his hands rove higher.

She giggled, either from nerves or anticipation, he couldn't be sure. "Are you out of your mind?"

"Probably." He let his fingers play with the lace and slowly edged higher. Her nipples were already puckered and he plucked them.

"Ah." She wrapped her arms around his neck and arched her breasts into his eager hands. "Are you saying I'm kissing an insane man?"

"One who's crazy about you." He tweaked her nipples and enjoyed her soft moan of desire.

"Mmm." She raised her lips to his. "How come you're so warm and I'm so cold?"

"That would be my fault."

"Oh, really."

"Darling, I unbuttoned your jacket."

She looked down, then back at him in amazement. "When did you—"

"You'll have to allow me to keep some secrets." He nuzzled her ear and bent his head to the opening. Very slowly, he ran his tongue from her throat down the V of her collar, inching back the denim just an inch.

She trembled and guided his head to her breasts. "I thought you were going to kiss me. Now you'll have to warm me up."

"Actually, I said you should kiss me." He straightened, placed both hands on her waist, then let his palms slide upwards, stopping on her rib cage, just below her bra, his fingers busily caressing, teasing and tweaking her nipples. "And I'll be happy to warm you up."

"It's about time," she complained, her tone husky.

He cupped her through the lace, allowed his fingers to spread slowly over her breasts. She trembled beneath his touch but she didn't back away—just the opposite. She arched her back and pressed against him, like a woman who knew exactly what she wanted.

Reaching up behind his head, she tugged his mouth down to hers until their lips were just inches apart. "You realize I don't usually kiss a guy on the first day, however, I suppose in your case I can make an exception."

"Because I'm exceptional?" His thumbs flicked back and forth over her nipples.

She let out another soft moan of desire. "Because we've already been naked together, and because you're exceptionally bad."

He tweaked her nipples a little harder, pleased as

the little nubs remained rock-hard. "So you like bad?"

"I like you, Jason. I don't trust you worth a damn. But I like you." And after making that pronouncement, she kissed him, eagerly, opening her mouth, giving him free reign to pluck and pinch and pleasure her breasts.

He pulled his mouth away to nuzzle her ear. "Your skin is so soft and smooth." He understood the fine line that created pleasure and didn't want to step over it. "How do my hands feel?"

"Hot."

"You aren't cold anymore?"

She shook her head. In the moonlight, as he withdraw his hands and rebuttoned her jacket, disappointment clouded her eyes. *Good.*

If Jason was any judge of women, and he considered himself an artist with the female sex, Kimberly had been ready to make love to him back in the hotel room. While she was far from the sophisticated woman of the world he usually pursued, the sparks between them were undeniable. With his determination to go slowly, sweat had broken out on his brow, but he was fairly certain that she now wanted him just as much as he wanted her.

While he could play her body as easily as he could pick a lock, he wanted her to hand him the key. So he would be patient, even if the seam of his slacks felt as though it might pop.

However, he could only take so much at a time, and her bold kiss and responsive breasts had him ready to abduct her to the nearest castle and make her his prisoner. He took her hand again and tried not to

think how he'd rather be touching her oh-so-wonderful breasts, tweaking her delectable nipples.

He forced enthusiasm into his tone. "Come on. Our kayak's waiting."

She strolled beside him, her voice curious, with remnants of husky need. "And when did you arrange for a kayak?"

He could hardly tell her that he'd phoned the Shey Group right before he'd come to her room. Logan Kincaid had contacts all over the world. To a man like him, arranging for a kayak to be waiting at the end of the quay was done as easily as most men parked their car in the garage. But Jason wasn't about to admit his connection to the secret group of men who took on high-tech missions for their government as well as corporate America. So he lied.

"I was hoping to take an early-morning trip along the shoreline. See some nature."

"In a *two*-person kayak?"

They'd reached the dock where the kayak floated, bobbing gently in the calm harbor. Two paddles and two life jackets could be clearly seen.

"Why don't I believe you?"

Because she had good instincts.

Instead, he said, "I have no idea." He led her out onto the dock, plucked the life jacket from the craft and handed it to her.

He took a moment to study the midnight shadows. Right now the area appeared deserted. The tourist booth that sold boat rides to a nearby island was closed up tight. It was still too early for the fishing boats to head out to sea.

In the harbor, sail-and-motor boats turned into a light breeze, their bows all pointing northward. Seagulls slept atop upright dock posts and waves lapped against the rock shore. Every indication was one of quiet and peace.

Yet, a sixth sense told Jason that someone else was out here. And that someone was taking more than a casual interest in their activities.

He saw no one. But he trusted his instincts.

Kimberly clicked the life-jacket straps shut and picked up the paddle. "It's lighter than I expected."

"You'll do fine. Step into the center of the boat and ease into the seat slowly."

She eyed the narrow watercraft warily. "Suppose it tips?"

"We'll get wet." He stepped into the back seat where he could steer most easily and sank to the seat, prepared to counterbalance her weight if necessary.

She lowered herself to the seat lightly. When she wasn't nervous around men, her clumsiness disappeared, so her natural balance and grace didn't surprise him. With those lithe curves, her body was made for...athletic activity. And he knew just what kind of activity would suit him best—and it damn sure wasn't paddling a kayak.

He shoved off, amused but not surprised that his thoughts kept turning to sex. He hadn't been around a woman who intrigued him as much as Kimberly in a long time. He found her combination of sass and reluctance refreshing. He admired that she remained suspicious of him and yet dared to plunge into a relationship. And although she'd let him take the lead in tonight's adventure, he suspected that if he made

one wrong move, she wouldn't hesitate to set him straight.

Heading toward the harbor's mouth, he still hugged the shoreline where rows of cottages and small hotels dotted the scenery of thickly wooded areas. He heard no voices, no boat engines. Not even a car.

"Dip one end of the paddle, then the other. I'll match your rhythm. If you get tired, feel free to rest."

She grunted and he could sense her concentrating. It didn't take her long to catch on. Soon the kayak was skimming over the surface.

Between paddle strokes, she spoke in a normal tone. "Are we staying so close to shore in case we tip?"

"Voices can carry a surprisingly long way over the water," he warned her, then answered her question. "But we're hugging the shoreline so I can stop to answer a call of nature." Another lie. They rolled off his tongue so easily, and she would soon learn about this one—but there was no help for it, unless he wanted to inform those watching him of his plans— which he most definitely didn't.

When he found a likely landing spot, he steered the craft toward the rocky shore. When the bow touched the beach, he waded to land, merged into the shadows, then returned after a suitable amount of time with two large rocks, one hidden in each hand. From a distance, in the darkness, any curious onlookers would remain unaware of his activity.

Up close, Kimberly was about to comment. "Jason—"

"Shh, darling." He leaned over and planted a kiss on her mouth, then pulled back, amazed at how dif-

ficult it had been not to deepen the kiss. "You'll have what you want soon enough."

After gently placing the rocks inside the boat, he turned the kayak around, floated it into knee-deep water, then climbed aboard. He steered around the harbor's jetty and the wind kicked up. Tiny whitecaps rolled atop cresting waves. He pointed into the wind. "Can you keep us headed that way?"

"I'll try."

Now that they were out of sight of land, he removed his jacket and unwound her wet navy suit that he'd wrapped around his arm. From a pocket, he took out the incriminating wig. He kept everything in his lap and tied the suit and wig around the rocks. Using a minimum of motion, he dumped it all overboard under the guise of rinsing his hands in the sea.

He resumed his seat. "We're all set. If you want, we can turn back now."

From atop the jetty, a flashlight suddenly shone out of the darkness. A man's voice blared over a bullhorn. "Ahoy the boat."

"Something we can do for you?" Jason called out, pleased that the suit and wig had sunk so quickly. Unless someone immediately dragged the sea bottom, an expensive and time-consuming proposition, Kimberly had nothing to worry about.

"This is the police." At the order Kimberly froze in the seat in front of him. "Please return to the dock immediately."

"Is something wrong?" Jason asked, paddling steadily, heading back to shore.

Kimberly looked over her shoulder at him and whispered, "Could they have—"

"No. I suspect this is just a routine inspection. In the States, the U.S. Coast Guard stops watercrafts all the time. Maybe they just want to check our life jackets. It's possible they suspect we're smuggling, but highly unlikely that they're working with the police investigation on the stolen book."

Kimberly sighed and started to paddle again. "And maybe they think you're James Bond—not that I'm complaining."

He grinned at her sarcasm. "I'll think of a way for you to thank me later."

She chuckled, her laughter warm and husky. "I'll look forward to it."

JASON TOOK CARE of the authorities' questions in the same smooth manner he took care of everything else. They'd asked simple questions like where they'd come from and where they were headed before letting them go about their business.

After Kimberly had debarked the kayak, Jason had flipped it over, soaking himself and partially filling the small craft with seawater. She was fairly certain he'd done so deliberately.

But why?

She hadn't had a chance to ask him until they'd left the inquisitive policemen behind and headed back up the cobblestone road to the hotel. Without a blouse under her jacket, she shivered slightly in the nippy night air. In his wet clothes, Jason must have been freezing.

"Are you cold?"

"That depends," he teased.

"On what?"

"Whether or not you're offering to warm me up."

She sighed. "The police kind of put a damper on my mood."

A few weeks ago, she'd been stopped by customs when she'd tried to smuggle those rocks in her bra. And now look at all the trouble she'd gotten into by researching how to steal the *Book of Celts*. She had to think like a criminal when she was completely innocent, a thought process that she found much more natural when she was at her keyboard writing about her characters, instead of when living her own life.

She was glad that she needn't think about any of the suspense elements of her script for a few more days. However, she still had to add those love scenes that Quinn had requested. She recalled the delicious foot massage during her bath and realized that Jason had thrown enough kinks in her plans to shred her normal inhibitions.

But now commonsense had been restored—funny how quickly that occurred when the man wasn't kissing her or touching her. The practical side of her nature once again had her weighing the pros and cons of pursuing the notion of having a European fling with the mysterious and sensuous Jason Parker.

Did she want to make love to him?

Yes.

When he kissed her, he made her forget that they had known one another for less than twenty-four hours. When he held her in his arms, her thoughts centered on making love. In fact, around him, she seemed to have a permanent case of shortness of breath and pulse-pounding tension of the sexual va-

riety. Her body's response to his was bold, brazen, burning.

But her brain kept telling her that no matter how many times Jason had saved her today, he was a stranger, with motives she couldn't determine. She didn't buy his oh-so-flattering lust-at-first-sight story that he'd agreed to accompany her and be her lover merely because Quinn had shown him her picture. No man in his right mind would make that kind of a deal—maybe for a *Playboy* centerfold. Clearly, there were things he hadn't told her.

Yet it was hard to resist her body's demands to fall into his arms after the way she kept heating up from his attention. And he'd just helped dispose of evidence against her as he'd done earlier when he'd erased the security tape at the library—breaking who knew how many laws on her behalf.

Clearly, his protective instincts toward her were in full force. And she couldn't help liking how amusement colored the way he assessed her situation. Where Terrence might have berated her for being so careless about the suit and wig, Jason hadn't once criticized or complained. Instead, he seemed determined to use the opportunity to get to know her better.

But back in her room, the very moment that she'd been about to say yes to sex, he'd insisted on leaving the hotel to get rid of her disguise. He wasn't putting his own pleasure first, and she found that endearing.

"You mean all my hard work to become irresistible has fallen by the wayside?" he teased, interrupting her thoughts.

She ignored his question. Remembering they could

still be being followed, she glanced anxiously to the right and then the left.

"No one's following us," he assured her.

"How do you know?" Once again her suspicious instincts went on alert. For a movie consultant, Jason seemed to deal with the police way too easily. Her parents had had that same knack for avoiding trouble. She'd grown up hearing their stories, and she suspected those stories had fueled her screenwriting career. Maybe that's why she liked Jason so much, his air of competency in handling unanticipated situations impressed her. And yet his skills also made her leery of trusting him.

"I've always had keen hearing."

"And experience whether or not the police are tailing you?"

"I picked up a few things in the service," he told her in that offhand manner he used when talking about his past.

"Like what?"

"Sorry, it's classified."

"Which branch of the service—"

He shook his head. "Sorry. That's classified, too."

"All right." She reined in her aggravation. "Since you refuse to tell me anything about your past, let's stick to the present." She glanced at him to see if he would avoid making eye contact and when he didn't, she snuggled against him. "Why did you tip over the kayak? And, by the way, I appreciated you waiting until after I got out."

He placed his arms around her as if he sensed she needed reassurance. "I didn't want to risk leaving any forensic evidence."

"Huh?"

"Those rocks had dirt on them. While I could have explained that the dirt was from the soles of my shoes, not the rocks I used to weigh down your clothes, I still couldn't risk them finding any stray fibers from your suit—either in the boat or on my clothing."

"But since I don't have the book, don't you think those were extreme measures?"

"Lots of innocent people end up in jail on circumstantial evidence." His arms closed more tightly around her. "If you ended up in court and the police showed a jury those clothes, if the guard identified you and they proved you got in to see the book with a false ID, you could have been locked away for a long time."

"And you really think the cops would have searched the kayak that carefully?"

"It was a risk I didn't want to take."

"So you dunked yourself for me?"

He slipped his hand under her chin to look into her eyes. "Do I get a reward?"

She allowed her mouth to turn up at the corners. "You want more than my thanks?"

"Much more."

"Tomorrow, we head to Ireland, right?"

"Yes."

All evening her subconscious had been at work on those love scenes she had to write. And now the thoughts came front and center fully blown into place. "There's a scene in Dublin that I believe you could help me with."

"Is that so?"

"I was thinking about writing a love scene on the River Liffey."

"And?"

"Could you make the arrangements?"

"Let me get this straight," Jason shot her his pirate's grin. "You want us to make love on the River Liffey so you can write about it?"

"I thought that would give us both inspiration."

"Why do I need inspiration?"

"I was hoping you would be...creative."

"Hmm. This is where your two protagonists are playing chess?"

"That's the one."

"Suppose we change the game from chess to Go?"

"Go?"

"It's a board game. Each time a contestant's Go pieces are surrounded, the winner gets to remove an article of clothing from the loser. Sort of like strip poker with a lot of touching."

At the idea of playing out that scene, heat and anticipation spiked straight to her core. "That could work for me."

6

JASON ESCORTED Kimberly to her room, then headed to his own for a hot shower. If he hurried, he could still make his phone call to the States and catch Logan Kincaid at a decent hour. Actually, no matter what time he called, the legendary leader of the Shey Group would be as wide awake as if he never slept.

"Kincaid here," his temporary boss answered.

Jason had been previously assured by a Shey Group expert that the cell phone he used was digitalized, scrambled and in cipher mode, so he spoke freely. "I searched her room, thoroughly. She didn't have the *Book of Celts*."

"Maybe she ditched it? Or passed it on to a partner?"

"She's working alone."

"Have you been with her every minute?"

"No," Jason admitted. "But following her is a waste of time. This woman gets nervous and shows it too easily to be any kind of agent."

"Is it possible she's fooling you with her innocent act?" Kincaid picked up the nuances without him having to fill in the details, and Jason appreciated how sharp the other man was.

Sharp enough to be the only man ever to catch you, boyo.

Jason shoved that uncomfortable thought aside and considered how Kimberly had assumed the persona of Dr. Johnson as easily as she'd slipped into that enticing green bra, and swallowed back a groan of frustration. He couldn't recall the last time he'd wanted a woman this badly. "I don't think she's acting the innocent."

"You don't think? That's not good enough. In our business, we have to know for certain."

"I understand, but I'm telling you that I'm watching the wrong person." Jason wanted to break off this mission. Right now he had no choice but to stay close to Little Miss Innocent who turned him on hot enough to go off like a skyrocket. Jason preferred to seek out the kind of experienced women he was accustomed to. He didn't want to like Kimberly or admire her or worry over her feelings. He most certainly didn't want to form any kind of attachment to her. There could be no future in that since he was a man who played the percentages. And the odds swayed toward a hot fling and then a permanent separation where they'd return to their own lives.

But Kincaid didn't seem inclined to release him from this assignment. Jason tried again. "She's researching her script, just like she claims."

"The best covers are the simplest ones."

Like a master thief doesn't know that? Jason recalled learning that lesson at the advanced old age of ten. He'd caught the chauffeur who drove him to school rifling through his mother's jewelry chest,

which he'd pilfered from their safe. And Jason had found the shared excitement so engaging and addictive that he'd turned the episode to his advantage. In return for not reporting the man's activity to his parents, he'd asked the thief to teach him the exhilarating tricks of the trade.

An apt pupil, who had soon surpassed his teacher, Jason had had an outwardly normal childhood, but his nighttime activities had been what he'd lived for. Oh, yes. He, better than anyone, knew the value of a simple disguise. For years, his disguise had simply been the guileless schoolboy that everyone who met him saw.

On the street, he'd grown up fast and Jason had learned to read people. He'd suspected from the first that Kincaid had only told him what the other man thought he needed to know. For the U.S. government to have hired the Shey Group to watch Kimberly Hayward so closely, there had to be more information that hadn't yet been shared.

"Do you have *any* evidence against her?"

Kincaid must have realized that a man like Jason— one accustomed to an initial stage of intense planning followed by a quick adrenaline-high strike—needed motivation to stay on a case. Like an expert fisherman baiting a hook, Kincaid doled out a tidbit.

"Kimberly Hayward's parents died suspiciously in a scuba-diving accident when she was eighteen."

Jason winced. He hadn't seen his folks since he'd been eighteen, either. They'd had their hearts set on him entering the family business and couldn't understand why he'd chosen any other lifestyle but theirs.

Their lack of understanding, the recriminations, the fights, had chased him away. But he could always make a quick trip back. It wouldn't happen, but at least he had the option. "What was suspicious about the Haywards' deaths?"

"Both parents had implants under caps in their teeth. The pressure changes in atmosphere from a deep dive would have been too painful for them to have taken up the sport."

Both parents had dental problems? Jason didn't think so. "What kinds of implants were under their teeth?"

"Poison."

Jason let out a whistle, his mind analyzing and evaluating the new information. "You're telling me her parents were spies and died from the poison, but that their deaths were made to look like a scuba accident?"

"Yes. Forensics confirmed it."

"Does Kimberly have this information?"

"We don't know."

"So what do their deaths have to do with Kimberly?" The story Kincaid was telling him seemed so far removed from the woman who'd reluctantly shared her bath, the woman whose life seemed wrapped up in writing successful screenplays. The woman with whom he wanted to share a love scene. Just the thought of touching her again, kissing her lush mouth again, had him semiaroused.

And he didn't like it. It was one thing to go after a woman, have a fling and be done, both adults taking

their pleasure and going on their separate ways, but quite another to feel so protective about her.

Damn it. She couldn't be a spy. She was too fresh-faced and dewy-eyed, tugging at his emotions when he knew better than to let himself become involved. He didn't want to admit to himself that he enjoyed flirting with her, teasing her, urging her over the line into that place where the two of them could take pleasure in one another's arms.

"Her parents were the best agents the CIA had. When she was younger, they traveled as a family. They often used their only child as a decoy."

Jason had never caught Kincaid in a lie. The man might not tell him everything, but he was a straight shooter. Yet, Jason couldn't swallow that last statement. "You're telling me the U.S. government now hires kids to be spies?"

"Not at all." At Kincaid's ready admission, tension flowed out of Jason's stiff shoulders. "I'm saying her parents sometimes used their daughter to further their own careers and assignments. Government sources believe that her folks may have taught her spycraft."

"I'm not sure I'm following. Her folks were American. They worked for us, right?"

Kincaid hesitated, then answered. "We don't know."

"What do you mean that you don't know?"

"I suppose since they are dead, there's no harm in telling you that her parents worked for the CIA. But they also worked for Soviet Intelligence."

"They were double agents?"

"Triple agents, we think. But…"

"But?"

"Our government needs to cover all the bases. However, with most of the CIA's focus on terrorist groups, Kimberly Hayward is currently a lower priority. So the Shey Group was hired to watch her, and I tagged you for the assignment."

No doubt Kincaid's best men were assigned to more important missions, too, or Kincaid would never have called in the favor. While Jason appreciated his assignment, he still wanted Kimberly's name cleared. "Is she aware that her parents were triple agents?"

"We don't know. That's another reason why I need you to stay with her. While she's overseas, someone might try and contact her."

"Fine. But tell me why a spy might want to steal the *Book of Celts*?"

"That's what you're supposed to find out."

Damn. Jason hung up the phone, his thoughts whirling in a windstorm of possibilities. As far as he knew, the relic was valuable but held no political significance. It didn't make sense that a spy would want to steal the book.

Kimberly could be perfectly innocent, or she could be deceiving him with her guiltless act. The pieces of this puzzle didn't quite fit and Jason suspected that Kincaid still knew more than he'd told him.

So Jason added up what he knew to be fact. The *Book of Celts* wasn't in her room, but she could have been working with a partner. He couldn't vouch for her completely. However, if she *was* working with

someone else, her partner might very likely be on her tour.

Was that why she'd objected so strongly to Jason's joining their group? Had she feared that his presence would make it more difficult for her to meet undetected with someone else?

Or had her response been more elemental? One of a woman to a man? Kimberly would have to be an idiot not to recognize the simmering tension between them. And she was no idiot.

Perhaps it was for the best that Kincaid hadn't pulled him off the assignment. Jason could hardly wait for tomorrow.

ALL OF Kimberly's research into Ireland for her script hadn't prepared her for the wild places within a stone's throw of Dublin. From the back of the boat Jason had rented for their afternoon outing, she gazed upon miles of bogs interspersed with monumental peaks and big glens and cliffs that were crammed with tarns. Waterfalls cascading down rocky promontories flowed into the black River Liffey, home to trout, pike and kingfish. But as she took in the scenery from the open deck beside Jason, her mind didn't remain for long on the broad vistas or the deep draughts of mountain air that she kept dragging into her lungs.

Nor was she reminiscing about the fine meal they'd just enjoyed at a quayside pub. In Ireland the day's main meal, dinner, was typically eaten around 1:00 p.m. and they'd feasted on potato soup, Irish stew, fresh and crusty brown bread, thickly sliced and slathered

with butter, colcannon—potatoes cooked with onions, cabbage, cream and butter—and washed it all down with tea. And they'd sampled plum pudding and apple tarts for dessert.

Kimberly took in the scenery, but her mind kept returning to the love scenes Quinn wanted her to add to the script. Specifically the boat scene on the River Liffey. Following her script, titled *A Burning Obsession;* Jason had cut the motors and had anchored their floating barge. He'd chosen one of those lazy out-of-the-flow nooks in the river where time seemed to stand still. Ashore, sheep grazed the green grass fields. On the main part of the river and out of sight, the traffic passed them by, leaving them in the wake of tiny ripples.

"Ready?" Jason held out his hand to lead her to the forward deck. A table and chairs waited under a canopy that shaded it from the afternoon sun.

Was she ready? Kimberly had no idea. But she'd made up her mind that for once in her life she wasn't going to play it safe. She was going to enjoy herself. Her inhibitions would not stop her from being with a man as dynamic, charming and sensual as Jason.

She dragged in another fresh breath of clean mountain air, let it out slowly, then squeezed his hand. At the sight of the board game on the table, her mouth went dry from excitement. She didn't have to play, but she would. She could call this off, ask him to turn the boat around and head back to the Dublin quay, and yet, the challenging gleam in his gaze didn't just egg her on but proved irresistible. As did her elevated pulse.

"Are you ready to play?" she asked him.

She wasn't. Not really. She was already on edge, and she doubted she'd be able to settle down and concentrate. On the other hand, he looked as cool and collected as a world-class poker player bluffing a full house. And way too handsome.

He'd handled the barge with a skill that had amazed her until he'd volunteered that he'd grown up around boats. Hence, his interest in kayaking, he'd reminded her, and for some reason his pointing that fact out had jarred her a bit. But she couldn't figure out why.

"White goes first." Jason picked up a white stone and a black stone and put both hands behind his back. Then he held out two closed fists to her. "Choose."

She tapped his right hand and he opened it to reveal a white piece. "I go first."

"Yes." He opened a board. "When we are done, this board will be full of stones. The object is for each one of us to surround the other's pieces. Each time that happens, the winner gets to remove an article of clothing from the loser. And darling..."

"What?"

He shot her a charming, knock-your-socks-off grin. "I can't wait to see what color underwear you've chosen."

She stuck out her tongue at him. "You sound pretty confident. Suppose I'm the one who finds out what you're wearing?"

He chuckled. "Well, I think with your kind of confidence, we ought to place a side bet."

"Side bet?" Why did she feel as though she'd been waiting all her life for this moment?

"The winner also gets a kiss."

She frowned at him. "That means the loser also gets a kiss."

"But the winner gets to choose the kiss's location."

At his words, her heart rate skipped.

Kimberly couldn't believe she was going to do this. Or how badly she wanted to do this. When she'd written the script, back when she'd made plans to come to Ireland, she'd imagined castles and green scenery and a boat ride along Dublin's banks—but not in her wildest imagination had she envisioned a scene like this.

Especially in the warm light of day.

Especially with a man as coolly amused as Jason. His piercing look seemed to dare her.

The game had yet to begin, but she could barely think about strategy. She kept looking at Jason, taking in his dark blue assessing eyes, his determined jaw, that amused grin. And she couldn't help thinking how badly she wanted to remove his shirt. Yes, she liked the idea of sitting opposite him fully dressed while he—

Don't count your chickens, Kimberly, girl. First she needed a plan.

She tossed the white stone back and forth from palm to palm, considering the board intently. If she placed her piece on the edge, he couldn't surround her. Yet, placing her stone in the center would give

her more options. And what of the corner, the safest play of all?

Jason didn't rush her thinking. He seemed to enjoy her indecision, the amusement stamped on his face.

Come on, Kimberly. Decide. Surely the game couldn't be won or lost on the first move?

She placed her piece on the board.

Jason put his right next to hers. They played silently for about ten minutes before she saw that she'd fallen into a trap. He'd surrounded her white stones with his black ones.

"Time to pay up," he told her.

"Okay." She agreed, holding her breath as she waited for him to choose.

He seemed to draw out his answer, but perhaps that was her own heartbeat counting off microseconds. "Come here."

She stood, pushing her chair back from the table. Closing the two steps between them on rubber legs was harder than she'd imagined. He didn't stand, but turned his chair, spread his thighs and drew her between his knees.

And then he tugged the tail of her blouse from her jeans, taking every opportunity to trace his fingers over her sides, her stomach, her ribs. She had figured he would take off her shirt and demand his kiss. She hadn't realized that he was going to torture her with sensual overload as he did so.

The man was in no rush. He'd barely raised her shirt up two inches before she was eager for him to take it off. And that's when she realized that the winner didn't just get to remove an article of clothing,

they got much more, they got to caress and stroke and tease.

And by the time he finally raised her shirt to reveal her bra, she didn't know if she could stand the sensual tumult needed to play this game. But then she saw how his eyes focused through the lacy purple to her hardened nipples and realized that he might be turning her on, but in doing so he was also teasing himself into a world-class erection.

He hungrily eyed her lace-covered breasts as he pulled the shirt over her head. "How did you know purple's my favorite color?"

"A lucky guess."

"I'm going to claim my kiss now."

"Okay."

She gave her permission, expecting him to pull her head down to kiss her mouth. Instead, he reached out, wrapped his hand around her back and pulled her right breast straight into his mouth. And he sucked on her right through the bra, causing sensations so hot and intense that she gasped.

His tongue laved her nipple and she almost collapsed. And even through the pulse-pounding pleasure, Kimberly couldn't believe that she was standing on a boat in broad daylight, letting a man she barely knew take her breast into his mouth.

She had no idea how long he held her there on the brink of ecstasy. When the sensation rose to exquisite levels, she tried to pull back out of self-preservation, and that's when he nipped her, his teeth clamping down to keep what he'd won. And she thought she might just explode right there from the pleasure.

But she didn't. And finally, when he let her go, she had to steady herself by gripping the table to walk the two steps back to her chair. She sank into her chair, shaking the table. All the pieces trembled, mirroring her insides.

"I believe it's your turn," Jason spoke politely, but he couldn't conceal the husky desire in his tone.

If she'd thought concentrating on the game had been difficult before, it was almost impossible now. The damp material of her bra clung to her right breast and the light breeze taunted her even further, a constant reminder—as if she needed one with her entire body trembling.

"Right." She considered the board. Placed a white stone and then nibbled her bottom lip with concern. She'd made a mistake early on that would cost her another piece of clothing—and another kiss.

All too soon he was beckoning her back between his thighs. Knowing without a doubt that he would remove her bra next only made the anticipation more agonizing.

This time, he took even longer, running his fingers under each shoulder strap, tracking over the swell of her breasts, easing beneath the underwire. She could think of nothing else, except the certainty of wanting to be here with him.

She held her breath until he unfastened the hook, loosening the material. She longed to wriggle free but at the same time had the contradictory urge to raise her hands to cover herself. His eyes, hot enough to light the lace on fire, had her squirming.

When his fingers explored the bared flesh around

the half on, half off bra that just barely clung to her breasts, she forced back a melting groan. Kimberly had known desire before, but not like this. She had the powerful urge to scream at him to hurry up. To do something.

But she could barely admit her feeling to herself.

Finally he brushed the bra to the deck, leaving her bare from the waist up to his gaze. "You have beautiful breasts."

"Thank you."

"Babe, you are perfectly matched, wonderfully responsive and those two hard peaks are the prettiest set of jewels I've ever see."

She could hear the sincerity in his voice. "I feel—"

"Exposed?" he grinned with pleasure.

"Wicked."

He lowered his gaze back to her chest. "Do you know how good you look to me?"

"Yes. No."

"Good enough to eat."

And with that pronouncement he claimed his next kiss, swooping his mouth down over her left breast.

When she'd still worn her bra, his mouth on her had been wonderfully erotic. Now he was ferocious, nipping with his teeth, swirling her sensitive flesh with his warm tongue. She forgot to hold back a gasp. Forgot not to steady her shaking knees by reaching out and clutching his broad shoulders.

Instinctively, she arched her back, thrusting into his mouth. Her shyness had dropped to the deck along with her bra. Embarrassment disappeared in a haze of white-hot need.

All of her thoughts focused on her blossoming flesh. She barely realized that she was outside, in a strange country with a strange man. She only knew that the Irish air and Jason Parker had combined to give her the most delicate trembling deep in her belly and a dampening of need between her thighs.

"Jason."

"Umm."

"You do realize I'll get even, don't you?"

"Mmm."

"You'll have to sit there and look at my bare breasts."

"Mmm."

"I'm going to distract you."

"Mmm."

"You're going to lose."

"Mmm."

She said the words to tease him and distract herself from the sizzling sensations pulsing heat straight to her core, but then she realized that this game they were playing—no matter the outcome—would have no losers. Only winners.

7

JASON DIDN'T KNOW which was better, the treat of tasting Kimberly, or the wonder of looking at her. When he finally had forced himself to let her go, it took every atom of control not to swing her into his arms and carry her to the captain's cabin and the king-size bed below.

But he wanted to give her the opportunity to recover from his sensual assault. He might not have known her long, but he already knew how wary she was of making a quick decision. He didn't blame her for holding out, considered her reluctance part of her charm—except that playing touch-and-taste games with her had him as edgy as a rookie about to make a play for home base.

If he hadn't known better, he would have sworn that his blood boiled and his heart sang. Light-headed, he had difficulty remembering his plan to lose the next few Go rounds. He wanted her to have the opportunity to touch him, to learn where he was sensitive and where he craved her touch.

Concentrating on the game with her sitting opposite him bare-breasted made focusing on the little black and white stones next to impossible. And from the excited fervor in her eyes, she wasn't doing much

better. But he wanted her to take charge, to set the pace, to feel free to explore him—before he seared her right out of her skin.

Not that she was fragile. She wasn't. But even a man of his experience was wondering right now exactly how turned on he could get without going off. Touching her and tasting her had his cock protesting confinement and made sitting uncomfortable. But he wasn't about to give up the view—not with Kimberly sitting there so prettily, her breasts wonderfully aroused.

Damn, she looked good, with her pupils all dilated and her mouth pouting as she attempted to concentrate.

He just wished his protective instincts weren't warring with his need to take her right here, right now. He reminded himself that he didn't want to overwhelm her with the intensity of his lust. He wanted her thought processes involved too, because he knew it was important to her. He didn't want to deal with regrets later. He wanted her with him heart, body and soul. That's why the cooling-off periods their Go playing gave them were critical.

He needed to give her the opportunity to think about not just her body's reaction to him, but what she really wanted. Why he was so sure he needed to give her this time, he wasn't sure. But she reminded him of a gorgeous bud about to bloom—and no way would he be responsible for plucking her before she'd fully opened herself.

''Your turn.'' She spoke as if she knew he was

staring at the board and hadn't even realized she'd placed another white stone on it.

He grinned at her, deliberately allowing his gaze to sweep from her wide eyes to her stubborn chin to her perky breasts. "You're distracting me."

"Oh, I feel *so* sorry for you," she teased. She wiped her palms on her rib cage just under breasts. "And I did warn you."

He sucked in oxygen so hard, the whoosh of air made her grin.

"You know it seems to me that I'm not taking advantage of my...assets."

"What do you mean?" At first he'd thought she'd been speaking about the game, but he'd been very mistaken.

She placed her pointed finger between her lips, licked it like someone about to turn a page in a book or magazine, then held the finger just inches from her nipple.

He couldn't have looked away if a tidal wave had threatened the boat. Kimberly might have been hesitant to come here with him, but she certainly had spirit. He stared in fascination as her finger lightly circled one erect nipple then the other. And all the while she watched him, like a cat about to pounce on its favorite toy.

"You don't play fair," he kept his tone soft and even. Although he was complaining, his heart felt as though he'd just run a marathon.

She grinned at him, hesitant, but no longer shy. "You know the Irish have a saying, 'Hunger is the best sauce.' Are you hungry?"

Starved. "They have another saying I like better. 'He who follows his own will is king.'"

She chuckled, her breasts quivering. "Well, if you don't move your piece soon, I'm going to think that I've stolen your will."

With a groan of real distress, he forced his gaze back to the game board. Within five minutes, she had his pieces surrounded, and while he'd planned to let her win this round, she might have done it on her own. He simply couldn't think with her skimming her fingers between her neck and the swell of her breasts.

"My turn." She turned her chair and then she climbed onto it. "Come here, big guy."

He did as she asked and immediately understood that her breasts were inches from his mouth. But it was her turn to choose which article of clothing to remove. Her turn to take a kiss.

Slowly, she unbuttoned his shirt, each movement of her fingers and hands causing her coral-tipped breasts to tauntingly tremble. At least with him standing, his pants gave him a little more room, but he expanded further to take up the additional space, finding no relief after all.

She slid her fingers between the buttons, stroking his chest, making a production of each inch of flesh that she bared. And if her caresses alone weren't enough to drive him wild, her wanton display had beads of perspiration popping onto his brow.

"I didn't know you had such a wicked mind," he commented, pleased that his breath fanned her nipples into extended nubs that reminded him of precious pink diamonds.

"Neither did I." She leaned toward his neck. With her teeth, she stretched his shirt back from his shoulders, taking the time to nuzzle his neck, nip his earlobe and brush her breast against his shoulder along the way.

"Are you having fun?" He now spoke between gritted teeth. He didn't know how much more of this he could stand.

"Uh-uh."

Her mouth was too busy to speak, licking hot sparks of embers down his chest. She swirled her tongue over his nipples, exploring, exciting, extemporaneously working him over.

Her tongue on his other nipple drove him wild. He sank his fingers into her hair and tugged her head back. "You're supposed to pick one spot to kiss."

She shook her head loose from his hands. "I don't want to play by the rules."

At her words, he snapped from the rigid pose he'd been mostly holding, leaned down and swooped her into his arms. "In that case, I'm taking you below."

"No."

He groaned. "You don't want to make love?"

She remained silent, her gaze sweeping over the boat as if she needed a perch from which to dive overboard and escape him.

Surely she wasn't going to make him wait longer for an answer. Or refuse him? The excruciating thought didn't bear examining.

"I'm dying here," she told him. He'd read her dead wrong. "What about right here? Right now."

He raised an eyebrow. "On the deck?"

"Why not?" She reached behind his head and pulled his lips close to hers. "There's no one around except those flocks of birds and they aren't going to mind."

"All right, darling. Here is good."

But he didn't set her down. Not when her lips had finally found his, shooting his temperature off the scale. If kissing her could make him this hot and bothered, he could hardly wait to see what making love with her would be like.

KIMBERLY WISHED she could take this moment, capture it and preserve it for all time. She'd never felt more feminine, more wanted, more cherished. Making love to Jason felt as right as a wild run in the rain, or when she lost herself writing her screenplays.

The inevitable rightness of this time with him seemed all wrapped up in the sparkling green, the Irish air, the boat gently bobbing on the River Liffey and her melting bones. So many things seemed right to her. The way he'd likely lost that last round on purpose to equal out their love play. The way his eyes clouded with lust, yet he held himself back until she was right there with him.

And when he laid her gently on the blanket spread over the deck and she gazed into his eyes, she couldn't bear not touching him and drew his head closer for another kiss. She thrust her breasts upward, loving the feel of his rough curls of hair against her soft and sensitive skin.

She pulled back, enjoying the feel of her kiss-swollen lips, his ragged breath in her ear, his heady

musk scent that she wanted to capture forever in a perfume bottle. "I've never felt like this before."

He kissed her forehead, her cheeks, her nose and her lips. "Like what?"

"Like I'm wrapped in a sensual blanket. And that blanket is all you."

"Ah, Kimberly, darling. Was that a compliment?"

"It was."

He groaned.

"What? Did I say something wrong?" she asked.

"No, darling. Everything about you is so right—except…"

"Except?" she prodded.

"I just remembered that I left the condoms in the master cabin."

She bit his bottom lip. "Are you saying you don't want to go get them?"

"Walking in my condition isn't easy, but for you, I'll make the ultimate sacrifice. Promise me that you won't go anywhere and I'll be right back."

"That won't be necessary." She reached for her purse that had fallen to the deck with her blouse. After snagging the shoulder strap, she tugged it closer, popped the clasp and rooted inside. She came up with a fistful of condoms. "These come to us courtesy of Maggie."

He grinned lazily, smoothing back her hair from her forehead, then plucked a condom from her shaking fingers. "You expect us to use them all?"

"A girl can hope."

"In that case, I shall do my best." He ran his chin over the tender curve of her breast. "Where should I

begin? Here?'' He nibbled her belly. "Here?" He wriggled lower between her thighs. "Here?"

"I think you've got it," she tried to joke, but her voice came out somewhere between desperate and needy, wanting and wanton.

When he parted her thighs, slicked back her folds and found her with his tongue, she arched into his mouth. "You feel so good."

And then he slipped past her dampness, into her wet heat, and it took all her control to hold still. But soon she didn't bother, digging her fingers into his hair while his tongue flicked over her. His fingers played her like a magical flute and she gave herself up to the moment and the incredible pleasure he brought her.

"More, please." She murmured, barely conscious of her words as the powerful needs overtook her, carrying her onto a crest of desire.

He applied more pressure. "Better?"

"Ah...ohh." She exploded beneath his mouth, shattering into oblivion for a few seconds. "Oh, my." She came to, still enjoying the shimmering waves of aftereffects, his tongue still creating havoc with her senses.

She tried to tug him up. But he didn't budge, keeping his mouth busy, his tongue driving her wild. She hadn't realized she could orgasm again so quickly. But soon understood the wonderful possibilities as he built from the last peak to take her even higher.

And this time when she exploded, she lost all sense of self. All sense of place. All sense of time.

Through closed eyelids, she saw a multitude of ex-

ploding stars. And still his mouth kept urging her onward to a place she'd never been.

"Enough," she gasped as another orgasm rolled over her, leaving her marveling.

He stood to remove his slacks and shorts. She'd seen him naked before in the bathtub, but she didn't remember him being quite this breathtaking. His wide shoulders and powerful chest, his flat stomach and corded thighs with his very erect sex jutting proudly, stole her breath. And left her wondrous with the sheer pleasure of enjoying him.

She could no longer remember exactly why she'd denied herself, why she'd been fighting the need to taste and kiss and make love. At this moment, from the tips of his neatly clipped toes to his mussed hair on the top of his head, Jason was exactly the man she wanted.

Reaching her arms out to him, she guided him back down to the deck with her. Took a long, lingering kiss from his mouth before settling her hips beneath his, parting her legs and urging him inside her.

He took his sweet time, inch by delicious inch, until she stretched to accommodate him. Holding back cost him. She could see the effort to go slowly in a muscle flickering in his jaw, in the muscles tensing in his shoulders.

"You okay?"

She pumped her hips, demanding movement. "I could be better."

He rolled to his back, taking her with him. She ended up straddling him with his fingers caressing her breasts.

"Now you can take what you want," he told her, happily stroking her nipples.

She had never been quite this bold, but she liked how he made her feel, both feminine and sexy and revered. Every caress of his hands, every stroke of his fingers revealed how much he enjoyed making love.

She, in turn, reveled in his hard, smooth flesh and the tangy taste of him. In how his gaze found hers and locked on as she rode him, pumping her hips with an abandon she'd never known.

"Slow down, darling."

"I don't think so."

She moved faster, harder and he gave himself up to her, his only concession to her driving him over the edge was that she come with him. He reached between her legs, slid his finger over her slick warmth, until they both exploded, her, then seconds later, him.

She collapsed on top of him and it took several minutes for her heart rate to settle and her galloping breath to slow. "Thank you."

"No. Thank you. Darling, you were spectacular."

She felt quite naughty and sated as she snuggled against his chest, resting her head in the crook of his neck. The boat rocked under them and the breeze whisked their skin dry.

Kimberly closed her eyes, used him for both a pillow and blanket, letting him cradle her in his arms.

THEY MADE LOVE again before upping anchor and heading back to Dublin. She and Jason shared an early meal in a pub, then walked hand-in-hand gazing

into busy stores, their windows enticing with fine Irish linens, Celtic jewelry, European antiques and a bookstore on every block, reflecting the Irish love of literature. They brought fresh strawberries and nuts at an open-air market and munched as they strode along the crowded city streets.

With a happy heart, she watched street performers—a harpist and jive limboists—along Grafton Street, ground zero for tourists and residents alike. The city seemed especially delightful because Jason was there to share it with her. And she bought several gifts, an antique perfume bottle for her good friend Cate's birthday present, Irish chocolate and candlesticks for Maggie and fabulous silver Celtic cuff links for Quinn.

When they reached their hotel, Kimberly squeezed Jason's hand, kissed him on the lips lightly, her heart skipping with joy. "Why don't you pick up whatever you need and then join me in my room?"

"Sounds good."

When she'd left the hotel earlier, she hadn't known making love with Jason could cause this kind of happiness. They'd spent the afternoon making love, walked all evening and she wanted to make love again all night. She didn't feel the least bit tired. She actually took four flights of steps up to her room instead of waiting for the elevator, her feet practically skipping all the way.

She reached her room and unlocked the door, just in time to hear the phone ringing. After tossing her packages onto the bed, she breathlessly hurried to the phone, expecting to hear Jason's voice on the line.

An Important Message from the Editors

Dear Reader,

Because you've chosen to read one of our fine romance novels, we'd like to say "thank you!" And, as a special way to thank you, we've selected two more of the books you love so well, plus an exciting Mystery Gift, to send you absolutely FREE!

Please enjoy them with our compliments...

Pam Powers

Peel off Seal and Place Inside...

FREE GIFT SEAL
EDITOR'S
THANK YOU

How to validate your Editor's
FREE GIFT
"Thank You"

1. Peel off gift seal from front cover. Place it in space provided at right. This automatically entitles you to receive 2 FREE BOOKS and a fabulous mystery gift.

2. Send back this card and you'll get 2 brand-new Harlequin® Blaze™ novels. These books have a cover price of $4.50 each in the U.S. and $5.25 each in Canada, but they are yours to keep absolutely free.

3. There's no catch. You're under no obligation to buy anything. We charge nothing—ZERO—for your first shipment. And you don't have to make any minimum number of purchases—not even one!

4. The fact is, thousands of readers enjoy receiving their books by mail from the Harlequin Reader Service®. They enjoy the convenience of home delivery...they like getting the best new novels at discount prices BEFORE they're available in stores...and they love their *Heart to Heart* subscriber newsletter featuring author news, horoscopes, recipes, book reviews and much more!

5. We hope that after receiving your free books you'll want to remain a subscriber. But the choice is yours—to continue or cancel, any time at all! So why not take us up on our invitation, with no risk of any kind. You'll be glad you did!

6. Remember...just for validating your Editor's Free Gift Offer, we'll send you THREE gifts, *ABSOLUTELY FREE!*

GET A *Free* MYSTERY GIFT...

SURPRISE MYSTERY GIFT COULD BE YOURS **FREE** AS A SPECIAL "THANK YOU" FROM THE EDITORS OF HARLEQUIN

Visit us online at
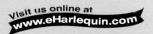
www.eHarlequin.com

The Editor's "Thank You" Free Gifts Include:

- Two BRAND-NEW romance novels!
- An exciting mystery gift!

PLACE FREE GIFT SEAL HERE

Yes I have placed my Editor's "Thank You" seal in the space provided above. Please send me 2 free books and a fabulous Mystery Gift. I understand I am under no obligation to purchase any books, as explained on the back and on the opposite page.

350 HDL DZ62   150 HDL DZ7H

FIRST NAME	LAST NAME

ADDRESS

APT.#	CITY

STATE/PROV.	ZIP/POSTAL CODE

(H-B-06/04)

Thank You!

The Harlequin Reader Service® — Here's how it works:

Accepting your 2 free books and gift places you under no obligation to buy anything. You may keep the books and gift and return the shipping statement marked "cancel." If you do not cancel, about a month later we'll send you 4 additional books and bill you just $3.80 each in the U.S., or $4.21 each in Canada, plus 25¢ shipping & handling per book and applicable taxes if any.* That's the complete price and — compared to cover prices of $4.50 each in the U.S. and $5.25 each in Canada — it's quite a bargain! You may cancel at any time, but if you choose to continue, every month we'll send you 4 more books, which you may either purchase at the discount price or return to us and cancel your subscription.

*Terms and prices subject to change without notice. Sales tax applicable in N.Y. Canadian residents will be charged applicable provincial taxes and GST.

She fumbled with the phone, lifted it to her ear. "Hello."

"Kimberly, is that you?"

"Maggie?" Kimberly sank onto the edge of her bed, grinning in delight. "Aren't you still in Tahiti? I thought you were incommunicado?"

"Silly goose. We brought a satellite phone to Tahiti, but this is the first time we've used it, and we didn't give out the number."

"I didn't expect you to call me in the middle of your honeymoon, but I'm not surprised that Quinn has gone to such extremes to keep in touch by satellite. I can't even imagine what this call is costing."

Maggie laughed her confident laugh that made Kimberly so glad to hear her friend's happiness. "Quinn can afford it. And I'm finding that spending his money is lots of fun, too. But that's not why I called, I've been worried about you."

"Me?"

"How are the love scenes that Quinn wanted you to add to your script coming along? He's not making you add anything that…"

"Nothing I don't want to add."

"Because my husband has a very vivid and imaginative mind."

Quinn wasn't the only imaginative man around. Kimberly blushed at how wonderfully Jason had set up her boat scene on the River Liffey. Their lovemaking still fresh on her mind, her skin still tingly from his touch, she wasn't quite ready to share. "So I take it the honeymoon is going well?"

"The water here is an unbelievable turquoise—you

don't realize how gorgeous it is until you actually see it.''

''I didn't ask about the ocean's color,'' Kimberly teased her friend.

''This island has one of those tiki huts built over the water. We can hear the waves lapping up against the foundation. Between the balmy sea air and the wave action, I swear it's like an aphrodisiac. But I didn't call to brag about Quinn. How are you doing?''

''I'm having a blast.'' Kimberly could tell that Maggie was wonderfully happy and wished her the best. Watching Maggie fall in love had been fun, but not experiencing some passion of her own made having her own news to share even better. ''I met Jason Parker and he and I hit it off.''

''I want details, girlfriend,'' Maggie demanded, ''especially the juicy ones. There have been juicy ones, right? Or are you holding back again?''

''Sheesh, Maggie. I've been here less than a week. And it took you years to go after Quinn.''

''That was different. He was my boss. Now quit stalling and tell all.''

''Jason's been helping me with my script.''

Kimberly could hear Maggie's sigh of disappointment all the way around the world. ''Kimberly, tell me why this man is different to you from any other or so help me I'll tell Quinn not to make your movie.''

Maggie's threat was empty. She'd never do such a thing and they both knew it. ''It's not that I don't want to tell you, but it's hard to describe him with words.''

"Try. You're a screenwriter. If he was a character in your script, how would you write him?"

"Mysterious, charming, with a dangerous edge. Protective, sexy—"

"Ohh, I like that part. How sexy?"

"Let's say I'm a very satisfied woman after a marvelous barge ride up the River Liffey."

"Wow. You really made love? He didn't get you drunk, did he?"

Kimberly laughed. "We weren't drinking." Weren't drinking anything but one another's essence. She swore she could still taste the sunshine on Jason's chest, smell his unique scent that made her want more of him already.

"I can't wait to tell Quinn. He's going to be so happy for you."

"Well, I owe you and Quinn big-time. Without you all I wouldn't have met Jason in the first place."

"I don't know Jason. What are you talking about?"

Kimberly frowned. While Maggie had been Quinn's secretary for the past four years, she didn't always know about her husband's schemes. Maybe Maggie didn't know that Quinn had sent Jason.

"Quinn did more than send me on a fabulous European tour. He sent Jason, too."

"I don't understand."

"Quinn didn't tell you?" Kimberly had to ask but she already knew the answer.

"Not a thing. If he's done anything bad to you, I'll wring his neck."

"Down, girl. Quinn sent Jason over to help me research the love scenes."

"What!"

"It's okay, Maggie. I don't know how Quinn picked Jason out as the one for me, but I'm real happy here, so no need to take any skin off your husband."

"Quinn!" Maggie yelled for her husband. "You need to come back here."

"Miss me already? Dying for my hot bod again?"

Kimberly grinned as her friend covered the receiver. But she could still hear Quinn. "Come on, Maggie. I thought we agreed. No phone calls. Now you break the rules and you want me to talk about work?"

Suddenly, Quinn's voice came over the phone clear and grumpy. "This better be important."

"Hey, Maggie called me."

"Don't remind me. She's talking to you when she could be nibbling on—"

"Quinn. I don't need that kind of information. So stop talking and listen to me."

"Kimberly, last time I checked, you work for me not the other way around. Are you giving the orders now?"

"No, sir." She sucked in a breath and let it out slowly. "I just wanted to thank you for sending—"

"—you to Europe? You're interrupting my honeymoon to—"

"Quinn."

"What?"

"Maggie said she didn't know you sent Jason Parker over here to check on me."

"That's because I didn't."

Kimberly's gut clenched. Quinn might be upset about his interrupted honeymoon but likely that was all for show. Still, he wouldn't lie to her.

"You didn't send Jason over to help me research those love scenes?"

"I'm sorry, Kimberly. I've never heard of Jason Parker. I don't know who the hell you're making love to, but I hope you're having a good time."

8

JASON SHOWERED, then gathered his shaving kit, a toothbrush, and a change of clothes. He patted his pocket to make sure he had an ample supply of condoms before locking his hotel door and heading down a fight of stairs to Kimberly's room. Barely refraining from whistling in happiness over thoughts of spending his first night with her, he'd ordered a surprise late-night snack from room service to sustain their strength and brought a bouquet of flowers.

He couldn't believe he was so eager to see her again after less than an hour's separation, but he felt like a college kid on a fancy holiday. Juggling the bouquet, his travel kit and clothes, he knocked on her door and wiped the grin from his face. He didn't want to appear overeager.

"Kimberly. It's me. Open up."

"Get the hell away from me."

He frowned at the closed door in total confusion. Genuine rage had broadcast through the door to blast him all the way in the hallway. "Kimberly?"

"Don't even try to pick that lock. I've blocked the door with a chest. You bust in, and I'll call the local police and have you arrested."

"But you invited me."

"Now I'm uninviting you. Leave. Vamoose. Scram."

"Kimberly, darling—"

"Don't you 'Kimberly darling' me. Go back and crawl into whatever slimy hole you climbed out of."

What had happened in the last sixty minutes? Either the woman was schizoid—though until now she'd seemed quite sane to him—or she'd learned that he'd lied to her. Disappointment washed over him as he considered how he had messed up.

It figured that when it really counted, when for the first time he really cared what a woman felt about him, he'd had to go and lie to her. Disappointment tangled with despair. Had he just lost her? And if so, what could he do to win her back?

She'd come to mean much more to him than he'd expected. The sophisticated women he usually dated had a tough veneer that Kimberly didn't have. He adored her enthusiasm, her intelligence, her passion for her work. And he loved when he could crack through her practical side to the passionate woman that she kept so carefully hidden from the rest of the world.

No, he couldn't lose her.

Could she possibly have discovered he was really a thief on loan to the Shey Group? That his mission was to investigate the possibility that she was a spy? He didn't think so—not unless she had powerful and well-connected contracts—which could mean she really was a spy.

Damn. He didn't want to believe in her guilt, especially after enjoying such a wonderful, almost mag-

ical afternoon. But what other explanation was there? The Shey Group hadn't sent him mail or left any phone messages. He'd left no trail for her to follow back to him, had had no conversations she could have overheard.

Working on a plan, Jason returned to his room, his thoughts scrambling to cover every angle. No way could he figure out the mystery without speaking to Kimberly. However, she'd sounded angry enough to stay miffed for a month. One clue gave him hope, if she believed a chest in front of her door would keep him out, she couldn't possibly know what he did for a living.

Opening his closet, he considered a multitude of options. Decisively, he stuffed his belongings into a backpack and changed into his working clothes, a black shirt, black pants, black rubber-soled boots and black gloves—but skipped his usual black mask. After slipping the backpack's straps over his shoulders, he strode to his window, examined the lock and picked out the tools he would require.

Opening his window, Jason slipped out onto the ledge. Usually he scouted every angle from the ground and the rooftop before he risked his neck. But there was no time, and when necessary he could plan while on the move. He looked down to chart his course, intending to remain in the darkest shadows. Heights had never bothered him, and normally he would have taken time to enjoy the view of the empty street. However, the anticipation of viewing the expression on Kimberly's face when he came through her window had him taking shortcuts. He tied the rope

to a doorknob, then swung out the window, rappelled down the building and landed lightly on her balcony.

When he raised Kimberly's fourth-floor window and slipped into her room, her eyes rounded in astonishment, then narrowed in rage. Her face, already white, went whiter. Her lower lip trembled, but then she lifted her chin and braced as if for battle. And when, with a smile, he pulled the slightly wilted bouquet out of his pocket and held it out to her, she slapped it from his hand, spilling the flowers to the floor.

"You risked your life for nothing. I'm not impressed with your juvenile antics. Now leave."

"Not until you tell me what's wrong."

She glared at him. "I don't owe you anything."

Her gaze slipped toward the phone.

"We both know I won't let you make a call." He closed the window behind him, then leaned against the sill, propping his hip in the corner and folding his arms over his chest to prevent himself from doing something stupid—like reaching out to her.

Clearly, she didn't want his touch. Stiff with outrage, she practically oozed indignation. "I rather think you should be the one answering my questions. Like how the hell you read my script?"

"Quinn—"

"Has never heard of you."

Uh-oh. Jason was careful not to allow his expression to change. She must have spoken to Quinn. Which meant she still knew nothing about the Shey Group or his real identity—but she wasn't going to

be satisfied with just any old story now. She was too smart, too suspicious.

Still, he felt a measure of relief in knowing she'd learned about his lie through ordinary means and not a contact in the spy community. Unless she was bluffing about speaking to Quinn.

"You said Quinn couldn't be reached by phone," he challenged her.

"They took a satellite phone with them." It didn't take her long to backtrack and put the missing pieces together. "You must have sneaked into my room—just like you always do—and gone through my things and read my script, didn't you?"

"Yes."

"You going to tell me why?" Her eyes flashed her annoyance to cover a flicker of hurt. "And don't you dare feed me any more of that I-saw-your-picture-and-wanted-to-meet-you crap."

"That part was true—except it wasn't your picture I fell for, but the real thing."

"Excuse me?"

"I'd been secretly watching you for a full week before we ran into one another at the library."

"You were stalking me?"

"Observing."

"There's a difference?"

"I never meant to hurt you. And I did like the way you looked."

"Come on, I didn't buy that story about your liking my looks the first time, I'm not going for it now."

"There's an undeniable attraction between us.

Surely, you feel it, too, or you would never have made love with me.''

"Don't talk to me about how I feel. I want facts.''

"I'm not supposed to tell you more, but seeing as how—''

"You screwed up?''

"—we made love—''

She rolled her eyes at the ceiling. "What's that got to do with anything?''

"—and I like you.''

"Oh really? Do you usually stalk the women you like? Sneak into their rooms and read their private papers? Make love to them and lie about all of it?''

"This is a first for me,'' he admitted.

"Sure it is.''

She paced, her shoulders square, her chin high, but he'd have had to be obtuse to miss the air of vulnerability about her. All that energy contained, except for her quick steps to the wall, then back, never stopping, but nevertheless pinning him with a ferocious glare of affronted outrage.

"Are you done yelling at me?'' he asked, keeping his tone mild. She had every right to be angry, but no one could stay mad forever. And whenever her rage wore off, he intended to be right there waiting.

She simply meant too much to him to give up. So he would stay and bear her anger, then try to pick up the pieces and clean up the mess he'd made.

"I'm just stating the facts.''

"At a high decibel,'' he teased. A mistake. She fisted her hands, and he could almost feel her fighting with herself over whether or not to try to deck him.

She didn't resort to violence, but her words shot out cold and hard as bullets. "Don't change the subject."

"Fine. Then let me finish a sentence."

"Fine."

She glared at him, and if her scowl could have sliced and diced, he would have already lost a lot of blood. But at least she was talking to him, and now that he knew what had happened, he could deal with the problem.

He considered several stories that he could have told her and discarded one after the other. He wanted her to know the truth because if there was any chance for them to make up, he had to lay his cards on the table. However, a good defense included a strong offense.

He gave her the most startling fact first. "The U.S. government believes that you're a spy."

"What?" Her indignation sounded real. In fact, he could plainly see that she didn't believe him now that he was telling the truth—or part of it. He shouldn't be doing this, but it was a measure of how much she'd come to mean to him that he was blowing his cover and his mission.

He uncoiled his arms and held them out, palms up. "I didn't believe them—"

"Who?"

"My orders are relayed through several channels, but I'd guess the original suspicion of you went from U.S. Customs straight to a low-level official in the Office of Homeland Security who checked with the CIA. They probably had a file on your parents and

decided you needed to be watched. I shouldn't be telling you this much but—"

"But you have feelings for me?"

"Yes."

"How inconvenient for you." She fisted her hands on her hips, her entire body shaking with fury. "And why should I believe anything you say?"

"Because it's true."

She sank onto the bed and rubbed her forehead. "Look, let's deal with one subject at a time, okay? You work for the U.S. government? CIA?"

He shook his head.

"Office of Homeland Security? FBI?"

"It's unofficial and less direct."

"You're British Intelligence?"

"Look, I'm not supposed—"

Her eyes shot a laser beam of angry heat at him. "But you're not in the movie consultant business, are you?"

"No."

"I need to know who you work for."

He raised an eyebrow, his suspicions back in full force. And yet contradictorily, he didn't for one second believe in her guilt. "What difference does it make which organization I work for? Unless you need to block a leak?"

"Very funny. Maybe I need to know which agency to sue," she muttered sarcastically.

"Now who's lying?"

"Whatever story you tell me this time is going to get checked out."

Now that was interesting. Was she implying that

she had contacts within the FBI and CIA? "Tell me. How will you check me out?"

"My parents worked for the agency. I keep in touch with a few of their former co-workers. Maybe that's why…"

"Why what?"

She let out the words on the end of a long, disgusted sigh. "…the government suspects me of spying."

"I was told you raised their suspicions by smuggling rocks in your bra through customs."

"How ridiculous. That was to test the plot of my screenplay."

"Apparently U.S. Customs agents were not amused. These days they are edgy and don't like being conned. Combine your little test with the fact that your parents…"

"What about my parents?" She turned even whiter. "Those bastards!"

"Who?" This she'd lost him. He didn't understand this new anger.

"My parents' handlers at the agency tried to recruit me a week after their 'accident.'"

The way she sneered the word made him realize she didn't believe the official version that they'd died in a simple scuba-diving accident.

"When I said no thanks, the handler vowed I'd be sorry. I always thought the words were empty, a threat."

"Does the handler have a name?"

"Brock Udell."

Jason took out his cell phone and called Logan

Kincaid. "I need to find out if Brock Udell, a CIA agent, still works at the agency."

"Hold please."

Jason stepped over the flowers and held the phone up so she could hear Logan's answer. He came back on the line within twenty seconds. "Brock Udell's retired and living with his fourth wife in Arizona."

"Thanks. Sorry to disturb you."

"No problem. That's what I'm here for."

Kimberly narrowed her gaze on his phone. "Who was that man?"

"My boss."

"He has connections inside the CIA?"

"Yeah." Jason couldn't keep lying to her and look himself in the mirror in the morning. He liked everything about Kimberly. How she faced adversity head-on. How her hair smelled and her skin tasted. How she gave herself fully when she made love. She deserved to know what she'd been accused of and who had sent Jason to watch her. "My boss's name is Logan Kincaid."

"My parents told me about him. He wrote some special computer code for NSA or NASA. He's supposed to be some kind of technical genius with former ties to the agency."

She seemed to know more about the man than he did. "Well, he runs the Shey Group. It's a private organization hired—"

"I've heard of them, too."

"Really?" She never ceased to astound him. Innocent Kimberly Hayward had a lot of dangerous knowledge behind her pretty green eyes.

"My parents turned down an offer to work for the Shey Group."

"I wish I'd been so fortunate."

She lifted her head and stared at him. "Excuse me? Don't you *normally* work for the Shey Group?"

"I owed Logan Kincaid a favor. Watching you is how I'm paying back my debt. However, he is paying me, as well."

"Why don't you sound happy about it?"

"I'm used to working alone."

"In the movie consultant business?" she muttered sarcastically, her eyes drilling him with suspicion.

He didn't want to go there, but was determined to come clean—so to speak. "No, that was a cover set up by the Shey Group."

"So what do you really do?"

"You don't want to know."

She frowned at him. "You work on the other side of the law, don't you?"

So she'd guessed. Better for her to know the truth than to rev her imagination into overdrive. "I'm a jewel thief."

"A jewel thief." She didn't look especially surprised or horrified. She simply took in his black gear and for the first time since he'd entered the room, a corner of her mouth lifted. "Are you a good one?"

"The best."

"And modest, too."

"You should probably know that I'm wanted on five continents. Thanks to the Shey Group's cover, the heat is off me right now. However, if you called the police, they wouldn't hesitate to arrest me."

She reached for the phone, pulled it onto her lap. "Maybe I'll just make that call. Is there a reward for turning you in?"

"Millions." He allowed an amused smile to reach his lips but his heart battered his ribs.

Don't make the call. Don't. Don't. Don't.

He didn't fear the police. He could be out the window and hitting the street before the cops took down her name and address. With two spare passports and plenty of cash, he could take the ferry to Holyhead, Wales, catch a train and cross into Scotland by morning and hop a freighter for the Orient before the cops got his picture on the evening news.

Yet, he'd never prayed harder.

Put down the phone.

She hesitated, staring at him in obvious indecision. "Why do you owe Kincaid a favor?"

"He's the only man who's ever caught me. And he didn't turn me in."

"Why not?"

"Long story."

"I'm not going anywhere."

At the knock at the door, he jumped. "Room service."

"I ordered us a snack." Jason strode toward the door, shoved aside the chest and opened it. He tipped the bellhop and accepted the tray, then set it on the nightstand. Meanwhile her unanswered question hung between them.

He really didn't want to talk about his worst failure, but at least she was no longer shouting at him to get out of her room. Straddling a chair, he took a seat

and faced her squarely. "I'd been planning a caper for six months. I had a buyer for the Star of Burma, a thirty-five-carat ruby mined in Thailand and smuggled out of Europe during World War II. The jewel was rare and in a private collection in Martinique. What I didn't know was that the Shey Group had been hired to guard the owner's art collection for the same weekend I'd planned the heist."

"Sounds like bad luck."

"Well, the theft went off without a hitch until I triggered a newly installed silent alarm—one the initial contractor whose plans I'd been using knew nothing about. Two Shey Group members followed me onto the rooftop to prevent my escape."

"That's when they caught you?"

"No, I always have another bolt-hole, duplicate getaway transportation and a spare passport."

"So what happened?"

"I jumped from the roof of the villa to the garage apartment next door. One of the Shey Group's men tried to follow me. He slipped."

"How high were you?"

"Forty-five feet."

"The other man fell?" she guessed.

"Almost. He was swinging by one hand, but it was obvious he'd broken the other hand in the leap. He couldn't pull himself up."

"What happened to his partner?"

"He tried to throw him a line but with only one working arm—"

"He couldn't let go of the roof to catch the line?"

"Exactly. I couldn't just leave him there to fall to his death. I helped him up."

"And that's when you got caught?"

"Yeah. Police carted me off, but Logan Kincaid pulled some strings. He told the police that it was a training exercise for his men, that's why I'd turned back to help and hadn't kept running because I was one of them. And since the jewel was returned to its rightful owner, I was free to leave. But I made Kincaid a promise that if he needed a favor...so that's why I'm here."

"How come you turned back and helped that man on the roof? Did you know you'd get caught?"

"I'm a thief. Until then, no one had ever suffered so much as a scratch during my heists. And don't make me out to be any hero. If I'd known I'd be caught, I might not have turned back. And then I wouldn't have made Kincaid that promise and we wouldn't have met."

"Why did you tell me all of this?"

"Because I'm hoping you'll trust me."

DID SHE trust him? Kimberly didn't know. He'd lied to her from the start and she couldn't suppress her anger at his duplicity. On the other hand, she wanted to fling herself into his arms and make him promise not ever to take such foolish risks again. She shuddered every time she thought of him dropping down the outside of the building onto her balcony as easily as most men walked through the front door.

"Tell me something, Jason."

"If I can."

In his black shirt, pants and dark boots, he'd dressed for secrecy, but it was his burning blue eyes that signaled his middle name should have been Danger. Sitting as still as a caged tiger, there was an electrical tension in the snap of his expression, in the set of his chin, in the angle of his jaw that spoke to her on a level she didn't even want to admit to, never mind analyze.

But she must.

"Tell me how and why you became a thief."

"The how is easy. Like many wealthy Bostonian parents, my folks thought children should be seen and not heard—and the less I was seen, the better." He shot her a mocking expression, almost as if daring her to challenge his statement and she couldn't imagine what kind of deviltry he'd gotten into as a child. Or how any parents could ignore the charming rascal. "So I took to hanging out with the gardener, the chauffeur and the chef," he continued. "One night during a celebration party to announce my father's latest coup in the financial world, I caught the chauffeur rifling through my mother's jewelry."

"Did you feel betrayed?"

"He was only doing what I wanted to do. My mother had magnificent jewelry—maybe not museum quality, but heirlooms passed down from European nobility."

"Your mother never let you look at her jewelry?" Kimberly recalled playing dress-up, using her mother's cosmetics, prancing around in her high heels, wearing her father's shirt that came down to her ankles, him teaching her to knot his ties.

"I wasn't so much as allowed in the master wing."

"But you were there to catch the chauffeur?"

He grinned that charming grin that shot straight to her heart. She could hear between his words, the ones he didn't speak. A child banned from the master wing? A kid whose parents didn't want to see him around the house?

Jason chuckled, reached over for a cookie, and popped it into his mouth. "He taught me a string of curse words I'd never heard before."

"And then?"

"I agreed not to turn him in—if he would teach me the trade. For a long time, we made a great team. As a child, no one suspected me of being a pickpocket. I had the freedom to scout out upstairs bedrooms of the homes we visited. It didn't take long to learn how and where to look at security systems and if I couldn't find one, I simply asked the household help."

"And they told you?"

"No one suspects children of wealthy parents." He frowned at her. "Don't look like that."

"Like what?"

"Like I was abused. I had the most marvelous childhood. It was challenging, exciting. Fun."

"What happened to the chauffeur?"

His face turned expressionless and his eyes darkened with regret. "Charles died of cancer when I was fourteen. He left me his picks and extensive library, a who-owns-what in the world of stones and the best electronic books money could buy. Except for a stint in the military, I've been on my own ever since."

"*You* worked for the military?" She couldn't imagine him taking orders.

He tilted his jaw at a cocky angle. "Every organization can use a good thief. You think only the Russians steal classified information?"

She sighed. "I suppose not."

No wonder the man had unbuttoned her shirt without her realizing it. Hell, he could probably remove her underwear and hang it from a flagpole before she'd notice.

She'd made love with a thief. A man who made his living stealing.

"What? What are you thinking?"

"I don't suppose you've ever thought of working for the other side of the law?"

He raised an eyebrow, his gaze twinkling. "Kincaid's hinted that he could use a man with my unique talents."

"But?"

"Until now, I haven't had a reason to change my ways."

"Until now?" She swallowed the lump that had suddenly risen in her throat.

"Until I met you."

Her heart slammed into her ribs and stole her breath. "What do I have to do with your career decisions?"

He winked at her as if being a wanted man on five continents was as insignificant as swatting a mosquito. "I might go straight for you, Kimberly, darling. At least while we're together."

9

Kimberly had never met a man so outrageously confident. She told herself she should be furious that Jason had lied to her. And yet, she couldn't help but admire his audacity. Many children in his situation would have grown up hurt and resentful of their parents' lack of attention. But the rogue had described his life as fun and exciting.

And in just the tiniest part of her, Kimberly was envious. Because Kimberly had always played it safe. Sure, she'd accompanied her parents on a few missions as a kid, but once she'd reached age ten, they'd decided she should stay home with her aunt. They hadn't wanted to risk her future, but had their insistence that she refuse all risks seeped into other parts of her life? Especially, after her parents had died in that "accident," she'd played by the rules and worked hard to attain her goals. Not until Jason had challenged her to try the love scenes with him had she ever really just let go and done exactly what she wanted—and damn the consequences.

And look where that had gotten her. Making love with Jason—a liar and a thief. In a gigantic mess. Her body lusting for a man in a dangerous profession like the one that had taken her parents from her, her mind

in a tangle of knots that had a stranglehold on her emotions.

And she didn't know whether to shout at him, slap him or sleep with him. All her life she'd felt as though she'd been in control of her decisions, her emotions and her choice of partners, but had she played it safe because her parents had asked that of her? Was safe and practical the way she wanted to remain? She was way out of her box here, so far she didn't know if she could ever be the same again. And changing terrified her, especially because she found it so appealing.

Despite the lies and heartache, she didn't regret making love with him this afternoon. And now the passion between them had erupted into anger—at him, at herself, at life for throwing twists at her before she'd nailed down the premise. She blamed him for shredding her nice, safe compartmentalized life, for showing her that she found danger exciting. She shoved off the bed and stalked over to him where he straddled the chair.

"What exactly are you saying? That you won't steal while I'm with you?"

He nodded.

"And if we're not together?"

"Then you'll have no say in my life."

"If I send you on out of here, I won't feel responsible if you continue to break the law. That's emotional blackmail, and I'm not playing your games." She called his bluff. Pointed to the door. "Go on, leave."

"No." He popped a grape into his mouth. She

couldn't make him, and when he tossed her a grape, she automatically caught it. ''Go ahead. Eat. They're great.''

She hurled the grape at his chest in disgust. ''Fine. If you won't leave, then I'll find another room.'' Like that would stop him from following. ''Another hotel.''

''You need me.''

Of all the nerve. She pivoted on her heel, pulled out her suitcase and haphazardly tossed in clothes.

''You need me to pull off your research on stealing the Gypsy Rose Vase.''

''No, I don't. I have it all figured out.'' She'd meticulously researched her script. Although she'd never visited the museum in Wales, she had pictures, building specs and diagrams. All she had to do was verify that the item could be stolen the way she'd written the scene—just as she'd done with the *Book of Celts*. She frowned, remembering how everything had gone wrong. How Jason had rescued her. But she wouldn't need him this time.

Jason popped another grape into his mouth. ''Two months ago, the Welsh Museum moved the vase to their new wing.''

''What?'' Was this another trick? She glared at him, furious at how handsome he looked in black, angry that he could so unconcernedly eat grapes while her emotions felt as skittish as droplets of oil on a hot skillet.

''The new wing has upgrades. Electronics. Surveillance. Guards on every corridor during daylight hours.''

"But that will ruin..." She glared at him. "How do you know?"

"It's my business to know. After I read your script I made a few phone calls, did some research. As I said, you need me."

"Maybe I'll just call off my plans."

"There's always a way around the new systems. Luckily, the security is computerized and that's only as good as the programmer."

"And no doubt you know how to bypass the defenses?"

"I might."

"Since you're such an accomplished thief, how do I know you didn't steal the *Book of Celts*?"

"I only steal jewels."

Her heart sped up. "And you're willing to help me out?"

"Absolutely."

Folding her arms over her chest, she glared at him, not buying his innocent charm. "What are you asking for in return?"

"Why nothing more than helping you through the next love scene."

She should have known. She'd left herself wide open for that suggestion. And he was the kind of man who didn't just take advantage of an opening, he created them, then stepped through to claim whatever he sought.

She hadn't even thought about writing the next love scene, never mind enacting it. She needn't go through with this bargain at all. Just like she didn't intend to

steal the Gypsy Vase, she didn't really have to make love. Except that she wanted to.

She really, really needed to make love with this man until she didn't want him anymore. Why not take another walk on the wilder side of life? Take a risk? Make wild, passionate love just because she craved his mouth on hers, his flesh against hers? Somehow being far from home, away from everyone and everyplace familiar made coming out from behind her conservative walls a little easier. But she feared that once those barriers came down, she couldn't raise them back up.

Yet, here was the most handsome man she'd seen in a long time, offering his body up to her, proffering his skills. However, she wanted more than lovemaking, she wanted emotional intimacy. She wanted sharing and caring as well as X-rated lust. He was reaching out to her by telling her about his mission, about his past and what he really did for a living. And he'd offered to change for the time they were together. That was a start upon which she could build. All she had to do was say yes—and she could reach for everything her heart desired.

But, the words stuck in her throat. She had to be crazy to stay in the same room with him after what he'd told her. He'd violated her trust in the most fundamental way and…she wanted him.

She wanted to press her palms against his black shirt and feel his heart accelerate as she lifted her mouth to his for a kiss. She wanted to tug off his boots, peel him out of those snug pants and spend the night together on the big Irish four-poster bed.

She raised her hands to her hot cheeks wondering what the hell was wrong with her. She was tired of weighing and rationalizing and analyzing. She was tired of trying to think four steps ahead when he could think eight.

Before she could change her mind, before she came to her senses, she took a deep breath and let out the air in a rush of excitement. "Okay."

"Good."

And as long as she was so foolishly agreeing to this bargain, she might as well cast aside her other inhibitions. "We should seal this agreement with a kiss."

He tugged her to him. "I like the way you think."

And finally her palms were on that black shirt, his heat seeping through the cotton into her fingers. She clutched his shirt, yanking him closer, her eyes open and locked with his.

"Am I making the biggest mistake of my life?"

"Are you calling me a mistake?"

She didn't bother answering his question. "You'd better be worth it, mister. Kiss me."

JASON KISSED HER, the kiss all the sweeter for how close he'd come to losing her. It had been touch and go there, and for a while, he hadn't known which way she would decide. With her in his arms once more, he had the opportunity to show her that the decision she'd made was a good one.

He had every intention of savoring this precious time with her to the fullest. Kimberly was so different from the women he usually met. Cautious on the out-

side but full of a zest for life on the inside, she seemed a mass of contradictions. She rarely let down those walls except through her writing; her screenplay was chock-full of danger and excitement. And she was so careful to keep barriers between them—except when they kissed or made love. She was full of interesting inconsistencies that fascinated him as much as her delectable mouth, her green tilted eyes and her sunny smile.

He inhaled her fragrance, a mixture of soap and a feminine scent all her own. To him, she tasted like the most delicate ambrosia, and, as he realized again how close he'd come to losing her, he tightly and carefully closed his arms around her shoulders.

Never before had he admitted his true profession to a woman. That he had done so for her had shocked him into realizing that she was even more special than he'd believed.

He let his fingers trace their way up her neck and into her thick blond hair, and he reveled in how she pressed against him, boldly giving and taking until he was forced to draw back. Her eyes had dilated and the vivid green glittered like a black opal. Her breath came in gulps and the pulse at the delicate juncture between neck and collarbone beat erratically.

He considered whether or not to kiss her again. If he did, he might not find the fortitude to pull away, but despite their making up, he sensed she needed time to come to grips with all that he'd revealed. So he shifted his pack from his back and removed his laptop.

She watched his every move as if she'd expected

him to pull a rabbit from his pack instead of a computer. "What are you doing?"

"We only have two days in Wales. One for surveillance. One to steal the Gypsy Rose Vase."

"Remember, we aren't really going to steal it."

"No problem. I specialize. It's jewels that speak to me, not glass."

"Jewels speak to you?"

He unzipped his laptop case. "Each stone possesses its own individual characteristics; rarity, hardness, origin and beauty."

"From your tone, you sound as if you're speaking about women, not inanimate objects."

"Jewels are far less trouble than women."

"Is that so?"

"They can be appreciated, complimented and caressed with no chance of causing offense."

"True."

The amusement in her voice didn't stop him from drawing further comparisons. "Jewels can almost always be counted on in an emergency to hold their value and are usually judged by objective criteria."

"I rather thought beauty to be a subjective concept."

"You have a point. Precious stones are valued by size, clarity and hardness but also by a combination of fact and fantasy, history, fashions, superstition and reality not to mention those with fantastic origins which can have magical and medicinal properties. But we need to talk about the vase—unless you'd prefer to go after—"

"No. I don't want to do a major rewrite. Histori-

cally, the Gypsy Rose Vase was given to a lady by her Gypsy lover. It's a perfect metaphor to mirror the story in my script. Besides…''

''What?''

''Quinn likes the story the way it is. If I make too many changes, I take a risk of him changing his mind.''

''Does he do that often?''

She shrugged. ''Quinn is brilliant and decisive. And he knows how to put a project together with the best people in the business. This isn't just my chance to sell an option. Quinn has the power not only to buy the screenplay, but to produce the film.''

Her eyes lit up and her features animated. He enjoyed seeing the sparkle in her eyes, the way she was putting everything she had into this opportunity. He admired people who knew what they wanted and didn't let fear stop them from pursuing their dreams.

''And what happens if you succeed? If you make the movie? Then what?''

She glanced at him sideways. ''I'm not sure I understand the question.''

''You achieve your goal then what?''

''Well, that depends on what the movie grosses. If it's a box-office success, I'll have my pick of projects.''

''And if it fails?''

She shrugged again. ''I won't be any worse off than I am now.'' From the tray, she plucked a handful of grapes and helped herself to a slice of cheese. ''My work probably seems tame to you. Not like climbing

into five-story windows or racing over rooftops to escape.''

He fired up his computer and typed quickly. ''Actually, you may be doing some of that kind of work yourself.''

''What do you mean?''

''After I read your script, I took the liberty of ordering the museum's plans.''

She peered over his shoulder at the diagram on the screen. ''You ordered the plans? How? I was told the security system was classified.''

''Who did you ask?''

''The Welsh Historical Society.''

He grinned. ''I ordered these from a source over the Internet. Kincaid didn't even flinch when I told him the cost—he just said to buy whatever I needed.''

''How much did these plans for the new wing cost?''

''A hundred grand.''

''What?'' She choked on the grape in midswallow.

Concerned he patted her back. Her eyes teared and then cleared. ''A hundred thousand dollars?''

''I'm sure the man had to bribe several contractors or building officials. And then there's always the chance we could get caught and try to turn him in to reduce our sentence.''

''But we aren't going to do anything illegal.''

''Just having these plans is probably illegal enough to get us arrested.''

''But—''

''You want to argue or figure out how to pull off the job?''

She pulled over a chair and studied the blueprints. "Do you have the second and third stories?"

"Of course."

He didn't say a word, just watched her study the screen. Her expressive eyes narrowed on the page that showed the security systems—computer monitors at every intersection. Guards at each entrance and exit. A gated drive with a fenced perimeter. In addition there were heat sensors, infrared beams and dogs.

"It's not the Louvre."

"What does that mean?"

He tested her determination. "Are you afraid of heights or small spaces?"

"Look, this changes my script. I could do a rewrite but I'd rather try and fake my way in as someone legitimate than climb in through the chimney or through an air duct."

Clearly, she could read a blueprint and analyze the security system better than the average citizen. However, that didn't mean that she wouldn't panic in a tight spot.

"Exactly how much training did your parents give you?"

"What do you mean?"

"Are you going to freeze on me if things go wrong?"

"This is just a practice mission. We aren't going to actually take anything. So there's no reason to worry."

"What about the love scene inside the museum that Quinn penciled in?"

She winked at him. "I figured we'd play that by ear."

At the fire in her eyes, Jason just barely refrained from rubbing his hands together in anticipation. The profits might not be monetary, but he hadn't looked forward to a caper this much in years.

"DO NOT REFER to the Welsh as English," Kimberly read to Jason from her guidebook as they sat side by side on the train heading through the Welsh country-side. Although her intentions had been good, she still hadn't figured out what kind of innovative love scene could be enacted inside a museum. And this morning she'd still been thinking about it while they'd packed. The tour group had left Ireland before dawn, taking a ferry across the Irish Sea back to Holyhead, Wales.

During their train ride, Liam entertained the group with a constant stream of stories. "England solidified its hold over Wales with the murder of Prince Lly-welyn ap Gruffydd in 1282. Until late in the nine-teenth century, children were not allowed to speak Welsh in the classroom. If they did so, they had to wear a 'Welsh Knot' around their necks, which was passed from child to child—whoever committed an error. The child wearing the knot at the end of the day was punished."

Across the table from Jason and Kimberly and rid-ing the train backwards sat Professor Jamison and Trixie, his wife, who appeared much more interested in a game of solitaire than in Liam's story. Kimberly listened and looked out the window, enjoying the sight of miles of sandy beaches, grassy cliffs and dra-

matic mountains with footpaths winding upward toward clear mountain lakes.

The professor peered at one of the many crumbling castles they'd passed. "King Edward I designed a ring of spectacular fortresses to keep the rebels in the mountains—"

"I want to see the Gypsy Rose Vase, dear," Trixie interrupted. "Can you imagine how romantic it must have been for the lady and her Gypsy lover?"

The professor took off his glasses and cleaned them with a handkerchief. "Nothing but lust. She cheated on her husband."

"Is there any truth to the old legend, Professor?" Kimberly asked. She'd been fascinated with her research into the romantic story that surrounded the rose glass vase. Supposedly, when the nobleman caught his wife with her Gypsy lover he'd tried to kill them, but a fairy had wrapped them in a protective spell, whisking them away to another land. All that was left behind was the Gypsy Rose Vase which he'd tried to smash. Legend said that the vase's strength was a symbol of their love and could never be broken.

"A couple with the Gypsy's last name settled in Virginia in the early 1600s."

Caroline looked up from her astrology book. "Star-crossed lovers can't find happiness unless they dance under the full moon."

Alex snorted, but his arm went around Caroline's shoulders. Kimberly nudged Jason to look at the couple and whispered, "When did that happen?"

"What?"

"Our surfer dude has hooked up with Caroline the moon goddess."

"It must have been written in the stars," Jason joked, then glanced at his watch. "We should have time for a meal before setting out for the museum."

Kimberly barely held back a yawn. "We could go tomorrow."

"Food will revive you."

Kimberly did feel better after eating a tasty omelette. The group had split up, with the Barrs going to Snowdonia to visit the national park, Alex and Caroline hitting the beaches, while the professor and his wife were heading to the museum. No one mentioned touring together, so Kimberly and Jason made their way to the bus station alone, and it was the first time that day they'd had a chance to talk without fear of being overheard by others.

"Have you figured a way to avoid tripping the alarms?" Kimberly asked.

"Yes, but you aren't going to like it."

"Why?"

"We have to sneak in this afternoon and find a place to hide out."

"We do?"

"My computer needs time to break their encryption. And to avoid detection, it has to hook into their system from the inside."

Kimberly frowned at him. "And while the computer is decoding, what will we be doing?"

"Making love."

If she'd been eating anything, she might have choked again. Instead she tripped and almost fell face

first in the bus's aisle. But Jason's steady hand on her elbow helped her into her seat.

"In public?" The thought of making love with Jason so soon had her pulse rate knocking and kicking.

Jason grinned. "Quinn's notes didn't specify the exact location. I'm sure we can find someplace semi-private."

"Semiprivate isn't good enough. Suppose we get caught?" Despite her questions, the idea of making love to Jason had her anticipating an afternoon of pleasure, except she couldn't seem to prevent her thoughts from coming up with logical protests.

Jason placed an arm over her shoulder as they strolled down a sidewalk. "Making love is part of our cover."

"Excuse me?"

"If we get caught, who are the police more likely to release? Tourists who can't explain the reason for their presence after closing hours. Or lovers who got carried away?"

"You have a point." As she thought through his idea, she considered ways to write the scene. "But aren't we twice as likely to be spotted if we're..."

"You can't even say it."

"I can, too." But she didn't. Her thoughts kept jumping around, trying to get past her astonishment at the fact that without his touching her or kissing her or even shooting a sexy glance her way, she was already turned on by the idea.

What had happened to practical, always in control, goal-setting Kimberly, who always knew what she wanted and played it safe? Even after Quinn had sug-

gested she add a love scene in the museum, she couldn't really imagine it and that had made the writing impossible. But now, she was considering doing it. The idea shocked but tempted her.

The danger of getting caught combined with the thrill of doing something forbidden had her stomach knotting in anticipation. And she could no longer deny that part of the thrill was the risk of making love—with Jason, a man who could push her out of her comfort zone with a hot look, a challenging glance or an outrageous dare.

A part of her wanted to kick up her heels and keep up with him. A part of her wanted to stay rooted to the ground and refuse to take a step off the bus.

However, his I-dare-you glance had her stepping off the bus and almost colliding with Alex and Caroline. Kimberly stepped back just in time to avoid an accident. "Hey, I thought you two were going to the beach?"

Alex shrugged his shoulders with a sheepish grin. "Caroline wanted to see that Gypsy vase."

Kimberly and Jason lost sight of the other couple amid the booths hawking cold drinks and souvenirs on the way to buy entry tickets. The museum was in an old castle; the courtyard the main entrance and the new wing had been added with such care that it appeared part of the original building. The tourist attraction was more crowded than she'd expected, with visitors speaking a half dozen languages.

As the afternoon sun dipped behind the huge wall and left them in shadows, the temperature dropped. Kimberly shivered, cold on the outside yet warm on

the inside at the thought of what they were about to do.

She had no idea where she and Jason would end up making love. He'd seemed pleased with his research, eager to go inside. But as they crossed the moat and ambled past the thick wooden gates that guarded the castle, she realized that the stone walls had been built as much to keep people in as invaders out.

If they stayed past closing time, leaving again might be not just difficult, but impossible. And yet, all she kept thinking about was Jason. Where would they make love? A closet? A basement? A rooftop?

10

"WHERE DO you want to go first?" Kimberly asked Jason.

"I don't supposed you're interested in checking out the jewels?" he teased. "I believe they have an extraordinary amber necklace stolen from a Viking ship, and the Star of the North, a diamond brought back from South Africa meant as a gift for a king—but war broke out and—"

"We aren't here to see gemstones." She tugged his arm, leading him down the main hallway, sorry she'd asked his opinion. "Let's go see the Gypsy Rose Vase and then if we have time, maybe we can look at your rocks."

"There's no need to be insulting." His mild reply told her he wasn't the least insulted.

As they walked past exhibits of armor, weaponry and instruments of torture toward the glass exhibitions, the value of the items increased, as did the frequency of museum guards. She noted one uniformed guard at every intersection and casual glances revealed security cameras watching practically every angle. When she thought of the heat and infrared alarms, she wondered if they should stop before they'd even begun. Although Jason had reassured her

that his computer could override the system, she didn't feel as comfortable as she had when she'd researched the *Book of Celts* in the Cornwall library.

Jason spied a room marked by a sign Authorized Personnel Only. He tried the knob but it didn't open. In less than ten seconds he'd picked the lock and pulled her into a dark room that reeked of cleaning chemicals.

"Where are we?" she asked.

Jason flicked on a penlight that he carried in his pocket. "Janitor's closet. This will work."

"Huh?" Surely he didn't think she was going to get romantic in this smelly closet.

"Help me with my pack, will you?"

"Sure." As she pulled the pack from his back in the tight space, she tried to take shallow breaths through her mouth. "I sure hope you aren't thinking about making love in here because the smell—"

"I just want to hook into the electrical system." He bent, took out a screwdriver from his backpack and removed a coverplate. "Now hand me my laptop."

"How can you hook it in here? Don't you need a computer line?"

"That's the beauty of my system. The virus is carried through electricity. I've found a secret back door into any system that doesn't have electromagnetic shielding."

She didn't have a clue what he was talking about, but he sounded as if he knew his stuff. "If you say so."

"It's slow, but the virus will gently invade the mu-

seum's security and infiltrate the operating system. Infrared monitors and heat seekers will appear normal to the guards no matter what we do.''

''You're saying if we touch the vase, they won't know?''

''Exactly. Their alarms won't go off.''

''What about their video monitors?''

''The program creates a feedback loop of the vase and will keep sending that picture long after the vase is gone.''

''What about your laptop?''

''We leave it. It's the cost of doing business.''

''Can the computer lead back to you?''

''All serial numbers and fingerprints have been erased. I have an electronic trigger in my pocket to instruct the hard drive to crash once we're safe.''

He seemed to have covered all the technical angles, but she still worried. ''What about the real guards?''

''Once the museum closes, most of them will go home. We just need to evade the occasional guard making his rounds.''

She frowned at the black laptop. ''Where did you get that computer program?''

''I wrote it.''

She made an effort to keep her voice steady. ''Has it ever been tested?''

''Numerous times.''

''Has it ever failed?''

''Once or twice, but I've worked out all the bugs.'' He stripped a wire and twisted it to another one coming out of his computer then wrapped black electrical

tape around them both. "Okay. Let's see what we've got."

He flipped open the screen and typed, his fingers dancing over the keys. Outside the door, tourists spoke softly as they explored the museum.

"Look here." Jason pointed to a diagram of the building's wiring. "This is our signal." He used the tip of his pen to follow a red line that kept going around corners and advancing ever closer to the security room at the museum's core. "Once my signal reaches the central room, it will insert and begin to alter the operating system."

"Will it damage—"

"Not at all. Once we leave, the museum's system will be exactly as it was."

She told herself they would do no harm—not to the museum, the computer and security system or the vase. In her script, her characters wanted to prove they were the greatest thieves of all time and they returned every stolen item after their heists. She didn't plan to actually steal anything, but if they were caught, would the authorities believe her?

"And how long until it's finished?"

"About an hour." Jason snapped the screen shut and placed the computer behind a box of trash-can liners. "We're done here."

He flicked off the light, took her hand and opened the door. He exited first and after she followed, she realized why he'd stopped so suddenly that she'd bumped into his back.

A guard stood on the other side of the door in the

museum's hallway, frowning at them. "What were you two doing in there?"

Uh-oh.

She thought fast. "I was looking for the restroom." At the blank look in the guard's eyes she used the English word. "The toilet."

He pointed to the authorized personnel sign on the door. "You are not allowed—"

"Sorry, we were just leaving." Jason placed his hand on her waist and urged her down the hall.

"He didn't believe me," she whispered.

"Of course not. He thought we were making out in the closet."

"Oh." Her pulse rate was skipping frantically, but Jason appeared as cool as James Bond.

"Jason?"

"Yeah?"

"Maybe this isn't such a good idea."

He steered her into a room displaying gold crowns, silver tiaras, sparkling scepters and a sword with a diamond-studded handle. "You don't have to make up your mind for another hour."

At the glitter and gleam of the gemstones, her eyes widened. "What are we doing here?"

"Shh. We don't want to make a beeline for the vase."

"Why not? Won't we look like almost every other tourist? The vase is famous."

"That guard is following us. Look at the jewelry. Or at me—as if I'm irresistible."

"Sounds to me that no matter what I choose to look at you've just set up a win-win situation."

He chuckled. "That's the best kind."

She dug her elbow into his rib. "Do you always get your way?"

He winked at her, then gazed with delight at the Star of the North. "I'm not going to answer that question on the grounds that you'll use it against me."

She sighed and stared at the next display. "How can a necklace be both ostentatious and stunning?"

"You have a good eye. Those square-cut emeralds are at least twenty carats. The colors and size match exactly, adding to the value."

"The guard's gone." She tugged on Jason's hand before he gave her a lecture on every stone. "Can we go see the vase now?"

"Sure, but why don't we go through the Chinese room? Supposedly the wallpaper was painted by artisans and there's a ruby—"

"The vase—"

"Okay. Okay."

The display case took up one entire wall lined with black velvet. The vase sat on a pedestal, the lines simple and compelling.

She'd seen pictures of the Gypsy Rose Vase, but up close, the color was deeper, richer and more fascinating. Shaped like rose petals, the vase took its name from its design and color. Kimberly could almost believe a fairy *had* cast a spell on it. But the vase was trimmed with silver, and she suspected the strength of the metal had done more to protect the glass from breaking than any fairy spell.

"What about the glass case?" she whispered.

"The glass is glued together at the edges. A simple solvent dissolves the glue. Are we going that far?"

She shook her head. "I don't want to risk the air damaging the vase."

"Then we will have time to go for the North Star, too."

She knew the stone had caught his attention but he'd promised her that he wouldn't steal while they were together.

"I'm holding you to your promise."

His eyes glittered with satisfaction. "Then I shall hold you to yours."

He was referring to her promise to make love, of course. Although he'd just set her up and she'd walked right into his trap, she nevertheless appreciated his keen mind. Not many men could invent a new way to hack security programs as he had. In fact, she suspected he might be able to sell his program for more than he could ever steal—but she already knew money wasn't a major factor in his career choice.

He liked taking risks, and she liked taking them, too. She couldn't wait to see where and how they were going to make love. Every nerve jangled in anticipation as he led her down the hallways.

Tourists were slowly emptying the building as closing time approached. Despite her nerves, they strolled at the same speed as other tourists, doing nothing to draw attention to themselves.

Beside her, Jason appeared casual, except for his eyes that seemed to take in every doorway, every guard and security camera before moving on deeper

into the museum. With his stride even, his long legs covered the distance in an amazingly short time.

He steered her toward the right. ''The restoration of the king's and queen's quarters were completed last year. According to my blueprint we should reach the…yes. Here we are.''

He led her into a bedroom with a tiny four-poster bed decorated with an ornate silk coverlet, a massive fireplace, floor-to-ceiling wooden bookcases filled with leather volumes protected by curved glass. A security guard strolled past but didn't hurry them on their way. Just the sight of the guard caused her heart to pound.

Jason guided her to a tri-fold screen used for privacy when dressing. ''Ta-da. We've found the perfect spot.''

''Here?'' She walked behind the screen that rose eight feet from the floor and would certainly conceal them from prying eyes, as long as no one got curious and checked the space behind it. There was about four feet between the screen and the wall, enough room for the velvet sofa that had been shoved there. Cozy, but private, yet still she worried about the light from the windows casting their silhouettes on the screen.

''Stand right here.'' She positioned Jason behind the screen. When he moved, it was obvious someone was there. ''Hold still.''

''What do you think?''

''When you hold still your silhouette isn't that noticeable.''

''Let's trade places,'' he suggested.

She went behind the screen and he came out into

the room. She checked her watch and saw that they had another few minutes until closing.

"Take off your shirt," he said.

"Huh?"

"I want to watch the shadows on the screen."

Yeah, right. "Okay." She pulled her shirt over her head and dropped it on the sofa. She didn't know if it was the situation he'd created or just that she wanted him, but she'd never been this ready to make love—without a kiss, without a touch, without any warming up. Maybe all the foreplay leading up to this moment had been mental, maybe her body was remembering the last time they'd made love, or maybe she was just plain in lust with the man, but she had never wanted anyone like him.

"Now your jeans."

"Is anyone—"

"The place is empty."

"Okay. I'm unsnapping my jeans. Unzipping. Sliding them down my legs."

"If anyone comes, climb onto the sofa and hold perfectly still."

She had never done anything like this in her life. She wanted him touching her, holding her. On the same side of the screen with her.

"If you want my underwear to come off, you're going to have to remove it yourself."

"Does that mean you miss me?" He ducked behind the screen, but his footsteps had been so quiet that she jumped at his voice so close by. "Ah, is that purple? I adore you in purple."

In the dim light filtering through the windows, it

was difficult to see, and yet she felt self-conscious standing there in her bra and panties with him fully dressed. "You have some catching up to do."

"Kiss me first."

And then she was in his arms, her face tipped up to his for a kiss, the warmth of his chest heating her bared flesh. And when his mouth covered hers, she forgot where she was and why she was there. She focused on the heat fusing her mouth to his, the tenderness in the arms wrapped around her and the very distinct bulge in the front of his jeans.

She never knew exactly when he removed her bra. Keeping track of those clever fingers of his was an impossible task. Especially with her breath coming in ragged gasps, and her flesh all prickly from the cool air. But when he found her breasts and covered them with his palms, she was glad his mouth covered up her soft moan.

He pulled back and whispered, "Slow down. We have plenty of time."

"Who's in a rush?" she shot back at him, hooking her thumbs into the elastic at her hips and tugging her pants down just a smidgen.

"Take them off." His voice, hoarse with need, set her veins on fire.

She cocked one hip at a sexy angle and peeled them down another inch. She'd never done anything quite this naughty and she loved the way she felt. Daring. Feminine. And so ready for him.

"More. I want you naked."

She wanted to be naked for him. She enjoyed the appreciation in his eyes, the rasp in his throat, the

catch in his voice that told her how much he wanted her. And his wanting excited her all the more.

In one smooth move, she dispensed with her panties. And then he gathered her into his arms and laid her across the divan.

She started to gather him to her. Then froze at the sound of voices. "Uh-oh. Did you hear that?"

"What?"

"That."

"Sometimes the museum stays open late for special groups."

"What?"

He settled beside her on the sofa. "You're going to have to remain still. Quiet."

She didn't expect that to be a problem. She was practically frozen to the sofa, wishing she hadn't so indulgently followed her natural inclinations. At the sound of footsteps and voices coming their way, she wanted to reach for her clothes but they were trapped under her.

Jason didn't seem the least bit upset—but then he still had on all his clothes. She'd been listening so intently to the voices coming their way that she hadn't realized at first that his hands were skimming over her breasts, stroking and caressing.

"Hold still," he whispered and then his mouth settled over her breast, his tongue licking, his lips nibbling.

She couldn't move. Or make a sound for fear of discovery. Strangers stood less than three feet from her on the other side of that screen. And her breast

was in Jason's mouth. She lay naked and decadent, her nerves on fire and all she could do was…nothing.

It was totally wanton.

Yet sweet.

No, it was delectable torture.

And the fire of need burned through her veins like lava. She ached to shift her position, to direct his mouth to her other breast, to find release and escape from her prison. And yet, there was nowhere she'd rather be. No one else she'd rather be with.

Her nipple pebbled inside his mouth, and she never knew that so many nerve endings could be confined in one tiny oh-so-sensitized zone. By the time the group on the other side of the folding screen finally moved on to another exhibit, her thoughts spun fuzzily and her ears roared from the blood rushing through her like an electric current of raw desire.

She needed to be in charge, on top, in control and desperately sought to change their positions.

Using both palms, she shoved Jason back, dimly aware that he had yet to remove his clothes. And climbing on top of him would do her no good if she didn't get him naked. Fast.

Only her fingers seemed to have gone numb and clumsy too. She trembled as she tried to unfasten his belt, yank his shirt from his pants.

He did nothing to help her. In fact, he directed his wandering fingers over her shoulders and back and hips, creating more fumbling on her part. She'd never wanted a man as much as she wanted him.

If she'd had the strength to rip his shirt from his body, she would have done so. She shook with a

fierce possessiveness that had her throat raw and tight, her stomach clenched and a dampness pooling between her thighs.

Finally, she tossed his shirt. When she reached to unzip those sexy jeans, she bit back a curse. The denim at his hips was tight and the legs didn't flare. And she'd forgotten his boots. No way were those pants coming off unless she removed the boots first.

"Kick them off," she whispered.

He sat on the sofa and held one booted foot up. "Do it for me."

"Fine." She grabbed the heel and yanked. Nothing budged.

"You have to turn around."

"What?" she hissed.

He motioned for her to turn around and straddle his legs. After she turned, he touched her bottom and she almost jumped out of her skin.

If she wanted to remove his boot, she was going to have to bend over. With her feet planted on either side of his, he could easily reach between her thighs, caress her where she needed to be touched.

Without any hesitation, she reached for the heel of his boot and he fondled her bottom, drawing closer and closer to the center of her heat. She tugged on the boot and when it still didn't give, she figured he'd tensed his ankle to hold her exactly where he wanted her.

"You planned this, didn't you?"

He chuckled softly. "I'm pleading the Fifth. Wouldn't want to incriminate myself."

He ever so slowly teased seductive circles up the

insides of her thighs and she bit back a scream at him to hurry. And yet, she wanted this edge of pleasure to last as long as possible. But she'd never thought waiting could be this difficult.

She arched her back, trying to encourage him but he was a man with his own way of making love, his own pace, and he refused to be rushed. She bit her lip, tugged on the boot in frustration, bit back a moan.

"Jason, will…you…please…touch…me."

"I am touching you."

"Not…ah…in the right…oh…spot."

He placed his entire hand between her legs and cupped her lightly. "Here."

"Better."

She squirmed, but the pressure was too light, too barely there. Instead of increasing the pressure that would bring her relief, he'd only upped the tension, drawing her into one very frustrated woman.

And then another group came down the hallway.

"Don't move." With the tri-fold screen set on the floor and her bending over Jason's legs, the back of the sofa hid her silhouette. She couldn't be seen.

But that was when Jason spread open her slick folds with a gentle thoroughness that had her biting her bottom lip to contain a groan. He stroked her softly, slowly, so seductively she wanted to scream with the delight building inside her. Like a master mason, he'd laid a foundation of desire, and now every touch was like piling on another superheated layer.

Her fingers clenched his ankle for support. She clutched him tightly to steady her rubbery knees, and

her breasts kept rubbing against the denim of his jeans, making her hips want to buck with wild abandon.

Only she had to hold still. Take whatever he gave her without saying a word. Without murmuring so much as a moan. Her entire body was trembling as his fingers stroked her moist clit, applying just enough pressure to make her wild, but not enough to give release.

She had no idea how long he held her on the edge of orgasm, but physically and mentally, she'd never been in this place before. She needed him inside her, holding her, taking her. But that was impossible at the moment with his hips still encased in denim. She needed release but he wasn't going to give that to her. Not yet.

He abandoned her clit and slid one finger inside her heat. Automatically her muscles clenched around his finger, which seemed drawn to her G-spot like a magnet. And he kept that finger circling, building another wall of pressure that had her shaking so hard she wasn't going to be able to hold back.

He was giving her exactly what she wanted, driving her, pushing her, propelling her toward an orgasm. And every atom in her body needed that release.

He was urging her to the very peak and she couldn't take much more. But she had to.

Damn him. There were people on the other side of that screen.

She had to wait.

Had to hold on.

For as long as it took.

And every precious second seemed an eternity to wait. Each and every second he took advantage of her position. Caressing with long lingering licks of fire that had her frantic to go up in flames.

Finally the group departed. Desperately, she directed her shaking fingers to yank off one boot. He lifted his other foot and she ripped that one off, too.

Somehow, he lifted his hips while keeping his other hand between her legs. She wrenched off those jeans and his shorts. With his chest to her back, he nipped her shoulder and his hands gripped her hips and guided her onto his sex.

"Ah. You feel so good."

"I can feel even better." Then he reached around her waist to play with her clit again and she rode him like a wild woman. Taking, pumping, grinding and when she exploded, he had to clamp the hand that had been on her hip over her mouth to suppress her scream. However, his fingers on her clit never stopped seeking and her spasms took him right with her into a place where there were no rules, just mind-numbing bliss.

11

To Jason the pretend stealing of the Gypsy Rose Vase was anticlimactic, pun intended, after the lovemaking. He grinned at his own humor as he and Kimberly left the museum. Their combustible lovemaking had been a hundred times more exciting than simply walking down the museum corridor between guards making their rounds, entering the room with the vase and with gloved fingers touching the case, like Indians counting coup, and then leaving the building empty-handed.

However, his heart was far from empty. He'd enjoyed every second in that museum with Kimberly. She was more than enthusiastic, an incredibly generous lover, a woman who despite her protests liked taking risks. He'd sensed awesome passion in her from the time they'd met and she'd surpassed his wildest imagination. The only thing that might have made it better was lifting the Star of the North diamond. Walking away from the heist had been more difficult than he'd imagined, but otherwise he was content.

"You know all that exercise and excitement's left me starved," Kimberly peered into the closed restaurants and shops of the sleepy town. Not even the dogs remained awake to bark at them.

"At this hour, we might find a pub. And a sympathetic barkeep to make us a sandwich." He steered her toward a bar on the corner.

An hour later, their stomachs happy and full after wonderful three-cheese garlic toast and a few pints of beer, they returned to the hotel. While Jason didn't want to assume they were sharing a room tonight, he was hoping hard that she would invite him inside. He was using the key she'd handed him to open her door when she grabbed his wrist and stopped him.

"Someone's been in my room."

"How do you know?"

"I left a Do Not Disturb sign on my door."

He plucked the sign off the doorknob. "It's still here."

"Yeah, but it was crooked."

"Someone could have just brushed by with a wide suitcase, but it pays to be careful. Stand back."

Jason didn't carry a weapon, but he wished he had one now. He considered whether to call on the kid at the lobby desk for backup, recalled his short stature and slim build and decided against it.

If there was one thing Jason knew how to do well, it was to open a door and enter a room with stealth. Jason unscrewed the bulb in the hallway lamp, leaving them in darkness. He waited for his eyes to adjust to the blackness, then opened the door, stepped into the room and just listened. For breathing. A rustle of clothing. The creak of a floorboard.

Nothing.

Keeping his arm outstretched from his body, he narrowed his eyes and flipped on the light.

"There's no one here." Kimberly entered the

room, her gaze taking in the bathroom while he checked the closet.

"I thought I told you to stay back?"

"I did."

"Did I tell you the room was safe?"

"I didn't know I needed an invitation to enter my own room."

He frowned at her. "That's not the point. You agreed to follow my lead."

"I let you come in first."

She was deliberately being difficult, and he let it go. The room was empty. Although he checked under the bed, he already knew he wouldn't find anyone.

"Someone's been in here." She was leaning over her desk, rifling through her script.

"How do you know?"

"I left the script in my bag, not on the desk."

A prickle of suspicion razored up his neck. "You're sure?"

"Yes. And the maid service only comes in during the morning."

"Is anything missing?"

She checked the closet, her laptop, the antique perfume bottle she'd bought for Cate and the chocolate for Maggie, and the costumes she'd brought along. She stared into the costume bag way too long, sifting and inspecting the contents.

"What's gone?"

"There's a pair of panties missing."

"Oh?"

"Pink panties. You didn't—"

"No."

"Well, maybe I dropped them accidentally."

"But you don't think so?"

She shook her head, sat on the bed and rubbed her brow. "Maybe I'm just tired."

"Trust yourself. You're all you've got." He grinned at her. "Except for me."

"What's that supposed to mean?"

"When you live on the edge, you have to trust your instincts. And right now your instincts are telling you that something is wrong. So concentrate."

"On what?"

"On what your subconscious is trying to tell you. What do you see, hear and smell? What memory is niggling at the back of your mind? Don't discount your instincts. Focus in on details. Hone your senses. Use them."

"Nothing seems right. My clothes aren't hanging the way I left them. The shoe under my bed is slightly crooked as if it was kicked. And—"

"And?"

"The desk drawer is shut." She stood from the bed and approached the desk. "When I left, the drawer was partially open because I had a thought about the script that I didn't want to forget. I was looking for a pen and—" She opened the drawer. "Oh…my… God!"

He leaned over and looked in the desk drawer. A diamond sat in a sea of velvet. A very large diamond. A diamond that he recognized immediately since he'd seen it just hours before in the museum. "The Star of the North."

"And the *Book of Celts*!"

He closed the distance between them, his mind racing, sorting and discarding possibilities with the speed

of a computer chip. Placing one hand on each of her shoulders, he tightened his grip to show her he meant business. "We have a big problem. I didn't steal that stone. You didn't steal the book. So someone else did. And they're framing us."

"What?"

"We have to get out of here. Right now." He wrapped up the stone in the velvet, shoved it into his pocket, then placed the *Book of Celts* into a backpack. He stooped to scoop up his duffel of tools and yanked her out of the room. "If I'm right, the police are already on the way."

KIMBERLY'S MIND whirred in confusion. It didn't help that Jason's iron-gripped hold of her arm had her taking the stairs two at a time, then rushing down the dark street. Police sirens in the distance made her feet hurry and left her breathless.

When he finally slowed their pace in a park, she gasped. "I don't understand what's going on."

"Neither do I."

He led her to a bench and gratefully she sank onto it. "Why would anyone steal the *Book of Celts* or that valuable stone then leave them in my room? Why would anyone want to frame me?"

"Who else has read your script?"

Huh? Events were moving too fast for her. She'd come back to the hotel room feeling so good and relaxed after their lovemaking. Finding the diamond had been a shock to her system and since then, she'd been running on adrenaline. "What does the script have to do with—"

"It can't be a coincidence that the *Book of Celts*

just happened to be stolen after you pretended to take it. And now the Star of the North is stolen from the museum while we were there and then planted in your room. But why did they steal the diamond and not the vase?''

''It's almost as if someone is twisting the scenes in my script, rewriting it,'' she muttered.

''Museum security was only down for a few minutes. Since we were in the room with the vase, maybe the culprit had to chose, another target.'' Jason kept his voice low as they strolled through the park. ''So who else has read your script besides us?''

''Maggie and Quinn, but they're in the South Pacific.''

''Who else?''

''No one, but...''

''What?''

''After I made copies at the local printer, I came up one short. I only remember because I had to drive back to print another copy. I assumed it was a mistake.''

''Maybe your script was stolen.''

''That makes no sense. A screenplay is protected under copyright law the moment it's written. And I registered it with the screen guild. Besides, I don't see how this is helping. What are we going to do with the diamond and the book?''

''Logic tells me to ditch them. Throw them into the ocean.''

A cold knot lodged in her chest. ''But?''

''That's what whoever set us up would expect us to do.''

She scratched her head. ''I could call the police.''

"And tell them what?"

He had a point. No one would believe her. In fact, she'd be lucky if they didn't lock her up and throw away the proverbial key.

She realized that if she'd been alone on this vacation, she'd likely be in jail by now. Instead, she'd met Jason and his helping her had turned out not only to be necessary but the best thing that had happened to her in years. She might be on the run, in a strange country, but she felt safe with Jason. And she trusted him.

She snuggled against him. "So what do you think we should do?"

"As much as it irks me to admit it, I believe we need to return to the scene of the crime."

She shivered in the cool night air. The hard park bench in the chilly night air wasn't conducive to long conversations, yet she was reluctant to return to the hotel. "My room will be crawling with cops."

"I meant return to the museum."

She stared at him, wishing she could see his eyes in the dark, not following his logic at all. "Why would we go back to the museum?"

"To return the Star of the North."

"What?" He couldn't have surprised her more if he'd jumped into the fountain and sang at the top of his lungs...in Welsh.

"Look, you're being framed, right?"

"Right."

"So if the Star is placed back in the museum, no one can claim it was stolen."

"Wrong. It's not there now. A lot of people will

know that it's been missing. The guards, the cops. Whoever reported the theft.''

''Exactly.'' He spoke with confidence and satisfaction. ''We'll put it back. Slip it to one side of the display case where the stone could have fallen and been overlooked—because no one would be crazy enough to steal a multimillion-dollar diamond and then put it back.''

She recognized the excitement in his voice, his pleasure at the sheer challenge of making the attempt. ''And the *Book of Celts*?''

''We'll drop it off at the police station.''

''Why don't we leave both the book and the diamond at the police station?''

''Because I don't want the heat. My face is too well-known. If we put the diamond back, no one will be looking for a jewel thief and my face won't be flashed on every cop's computer monitor.''

She eyed him warily. ''Look, there's no connection between us and the stone. How come you don't want to keep it, or sell it?''

''Just because we can't see the connection doesn't mean our framer isn't going to create one.''

''That would really be sneaky.''

''Don't kid yourself. We're up against someone smart. Someone who could even have ties with the U.S. government agency which suspects you of being a spy.''

''I don't understand.''

''Well, suppose someone is out to get you.''

''Why? I'm not that important or worth all this trouble.''

''Let's look at the facts. In the last two weeks

someone in the U.S. government decided you were important enough to hire the Shey Group to watch you. When you pretended to steal the *Book of Celts* from the Cornwall library, the book was really stolen. And when we pretended to steal the Gypsy Rose Vase, someone steals the Star of the North and now both items are planted in your room.''

''You think this has something to do with my parents, don't you?''

''It's only a possibility.''

''Your theory sounds too far-fetched to me. My parents died almost a decade ago.''

''Do you know what they were working on before their deaths?''

''No, but whatever it was must be outdated by now. I can't believe that matters.''

''I'd like to ask Logan Kincaid to look into it for us. Discreetly of course.''

''Why don't you have him also look into the backgrounds of our other tour group members?'' she suggested. ''After all, they've been in the same countries and cities we have. And who would know our schedule better than someone in our group?''

''Excellent idea.''

Jason and she walked and he used his cell phone to dial the Shey Group and requested the information they'd discussed. Then added, ''Can you find out more about the circumstances surrounding her parents' deaths?''

He hung up the phone but his questions brought back old suspicions of her own. ''I've always wondered what happened to my folks but the CIA has a policy of keeping secrets from the families.''

"If anyone can access the old files, it'll be Kincaid," Jason reassured her. "He told me that they died from poison capsules in their teeth."

"I'd heard that, but never knew for sure if it was true."

"Who told you?"

"A friend in the coroner's office."

"Kincaid said their teeth would have prevented them from taking up the sport of scuba diving, that they couldn't dive deep due to air pockets that would cause pain in their teeth."

"That's true. But they enjoyed doing shallow dives. It still could have been an accident. Either way, I might never know the truth." She kissed Jason on the mouth, enjoying his scent, his heat and his company. His presence not only comforted her, he excited her, and the contradictory emotions had her wondering exactly how deep her emotions went toward this man. "Thank you for helping me."

"It's been my pleasure." He tucked her under his arm, carefully as if she were precious crystal. "I'm about to ask something difficult of you."

"What?"

"I want you to drop off the *Book of Celts* anonymously at the police station and then stay someplace safe and public while I replace the Star of the North."

She didn't want to let him bear the risk alone. And yet, his chances of success were better without her presence to slow him down. She couldn't climb walls like a spider. She didn't think she could jump across rooftops. And she had no skills to offer. She would be a hindrance. And yet, how could she stay behind, knowing the danger he would be heading into?

What's most important?

That he comes back safe.

And to give him the best shot at success, she had to let him go.

Every emotion protested the logic of making this decision. She wanted to be with him, share the risk. Yet, that was selfish.

Simply put, he was better off without her.

She stood and kissed him, fiercely, almost savagely, her demanding mouth showing him what she could not yet put into words. He held her against him, but this time his heat couldn't penetrate the cold fear slicing through her.

But for his sake, she wouldn't say a word. He needed to concentrate on his mission, with no stray thoughts about her to distract him. Determined to send him off with the knowledge of her confidence in him, she melted against him, throwing everything into their kiss, knowing it might be their last.

Ever.

Finally, she broke away, and he placed the pack with the *Book of Celts* in her hands. She was determined to keep her voice casual, determined he'd never see a tear spill down her cheek. "Be safe. Be careful."

Come back to me.

KIMBERLY LEFT the backpack on the counter of the police station without anyone seeming to notice her. Then she waited down the block for Jason at the corner pub. A light rain had begun to fall and the roaring fire in the pub helped to warm her chilled bones. One of the Beatles' old hits welcomed the patrons from a

jukebox and the house special was written on a chalk-board by the bar. While the scent of beer, soup and hot bread gave the place a homey feel, she couldn't think about anything but Jason.

The tables were empty and a few regulars watched a soccer game on a fuzzy television. No one took much notice of her and she ordered tea, then settled in a comfy leather sofa opposite the fireplace, her back deliberately faced to the clock.

Time would pass slowly enough without her ticking off each minute.

Although she'd tried to keep her worry from showing on her face, Jason had known her thoughts as easily as if he'd read her mind. He'd lifted her chin, looked her in the eyes and promised with husky confidence, ''I'll be back soon.''

She'd wanted to ask what time that would be.

She hadn't.

She'd wanted to beg him to at least allow her to accompany him part of the way.

But she hadn't.

She'd almost told him that she loved him.

And she'd chickened out there, too.

Oh, she'd rationalized away her lack of courage by telling herself that she didn't want him emotionally distracted. But the truth was that she'd fallen for Jason Parker. Fallen hard, despite all her practical reasons that they didn't belong together.

A professional jewel thief had no room in his life for a long-term lover. But her heart wasn't listening to her head.

And if he got caught because of her...

Don't go there. Think positive thoughts.

Jason had told her that he'd only been caught once—never by the authorities but by Logan Kincaid. However, under normal working conditions, he also planned his heists in meticulous detail. Tonight there hadn't been time for anything except a mad scramble and a seat-of-the-pants plan that could get him arrested. She wished there'd been time for him to call the Shey Group for backup but she knew he preferred to work alone.

And while breaking into a museum crawling with investigators and cops might actually give him a good cover, she didn't want to think about how many people would be after him if he was discovered. Returning the jewel would take every bit as much expertise as stealing it.

While she had no doubts about his competence, too many unanticipated things could go wrong. One guard in the wrong place, at the wrong time. One slip. One grunt. One hidden camera. Or a suspicious cleaning lady.

"Would you like something stronger?" the bartender asked.

"Just more tea, please," she requested, not even remembering swallowing any of the tea.

Alcohol appealed to her. In fact, she wouldn't mind straight bourbon or whiskey right now. However, she had to keep her mind clear in case Jason needed her.

How had she ever allowed herself to fall in love? The truth was she hadn't allowed it. Love had simply happened. She'd always thought she could choose who she would love—but she'd been so wrong about that, or she would have fallen for one of a half dozen

suitable fellow students during her college years, not for a man with whom she had so little in common.

Unfortunately, she had no control over this giddy feeling she had for Jason. Absolutely none. That special awareness when he was in the same room with her, the way she always wanted to know what he was thinking, the way her pulse sped up at the thought of making love to him, these weren't just physical responses. Oh, no. Her brain was involved, and so was her heart.

However, that didn't mean she had to act on her feelings. She could just finish her vacation and head home with her script and her movie career ahead of her. She didn't know if doing just that would be brave or cowardly, and she didn't particularly care.

She loved Jason Parker.

Practical, sensible Kimberly loved an international jewel thief wanted by the law on five continents. And as much as she ached for him to rejoin her right now, as worried as she was over his safety, she needed to get her head straight.

What did she want?

Jason.

What else?

A career.

Were they mutually exclusive? Did she have to choose Jason or her career?

Probably.

Even if he asked her to come with him, would she go? Give up her dreams and her promising film debut?

She couldn't do that. She simply wasn't willing to make that kind of sacrifice, nor did she feel as if she

had the right to ask the reverse of him. She'd seen him in action. He lived for the challenge, the danger, the sheer joy of pitting his skill against the best security and alarm systems ever created. Without that kind of challenge, he wouldn't be the man she loved, and she couldn't take that away from him and watch his soul wither under the guise of trying to become law-abiding—unless he worked for the Shey Group, but he didn't seem keen on that idea.

And she had no interest in becoming a jewel thief—even if he asked her.

What other options did she have? If she didn't participate and simply accompanied him in his travels and then waited while he performed heist after heist, she would hate her life. She couldn't imagine a series of endless nights like this one, wondering what was happening to him, wondering if he was safe or already in police custody. That would be sentencing herself to a life of torture.

So she loved him. *Yes, she did.*

But that didn't mean they had a chance for a future together. They could have the rest of her vacation, the rest of his mission. And then they would say goodbye.

"Miss Hayward."

"Yes?"

The bartender pointed to a phone on the wall. "There's a call for you."

12

KIMBERLY PICKED UP the phone, praying that Jason wasn't calling from jail. "Hello."

"Everything went down great." Jason's deep voice immediately reassured her and tension eased out of her shoulders. "Can you meet me at the twenty-four-hour computer center?" He gave her the address.

"Sure." She wanted to ask a million questions but knew better than to say much over the phone. Besides, he'd already answered the most important of her concerns in his first four words to her. "What's up?"

"Kincaid e-mailed the information we requested about our tour mates."

And Jason's computer was probably still in the museum's janitorial closet. At least he was safe.

Safe.

She'd been so tense that it took several moments for the relief to transfer from her brain to her lungs that finally breathed in a deep draught of air. He was okay. He'd gotten into and out of the museum without getting caught.

She practically skipped the three blocks to the computer center. Through well-lit windows, she could see

the place was surprisingly large and busy. Much too busy for her to ask Jason her questions.

However, when Jason stepped out from the shadows between two parked cars and onto the sidewalk, nothing could stop her from throwing her arms around his neck, burrowing against his warmth and kissing him. "I am *so* glad to see you."

He chuckled, kissed her and then led her inside the Internet café. Coin-operated machines at the front took money and spat out log-in codes. She and Jason found seats in the third row back at a long counter that housed a dozen computers, monitors and keyboards. Jason typed in the user code he'd purchased, gained Internet access, typed in another password, then downloaded his documents.

He had nine files. One on each of their traveling companions, plus another on their tour guide. Jason popped in a disk, saved the files and then pocketed the information.

"We can read that on my laptop," she offered. "We're going back to the hotel?"

"Absolutely."

She lowered her voice and slipped her hand into his as they headed out the door. No one appeared to pay any attention to them. "You think the police are at our hotel?"

"It doesn't matter. The Star is back where she belongs and the police will eventually return the *Book of Celts* to Cornwall." Jason's steps along the dark city road were jaunty, confident. He really enjoyed his work and she wanted to hear about his adventure.

"So tell me what happened."

"By the time I had arrived, the cops were mopping up. A forensics team had already come and gone, as had the museum's director and the head of security."

"Did they find your computer?"

"I don't know. Even if they did, it won't help them. The program would have automatically wiped the hard drive clean before they found it."

"So how did you get into the building?"

"I posed as a reporter, bumped into a guard and lifted his ID."

"And then?"

"I walked in the front door."

"But don't those ID tags have pictures?"

"I inserted my picture and a fake name."

"And you just happened to have false ID with you."

"S.O.P. Standard Operating Procedure."

"Don't the guards know one another? And have a checklist?"

"Probably, but they were distracted by a diversion. I timed some fireworks to go off in the fountain as I walked through the front door. In the confusion and smoke, no one questioned me."

She swallowed hard at the risk he had taken. "And then?"

"I had access to the security system, so I flipped it off, walked down the hallway and replaced the Star."

"You just walked in and flipped off the security system?"

He sighed in satisfaction. "Well, it was a little more complicated than that. I hacked in from an in-

side terminal. You see I've hidden my regular program inside a super computer that's housed—well it's better you don't know the location—at a major university."

"So basically you used the same program again?"

"Yes. Then I had to wait for it to work." He hugged her closer to his side. "This time the wait wasn't anywhere near as pleasant as this afternoon."

She squeezed his hand. "It's your own fault." The memory of making love behind that tri-fold screen seemed so long ago but it had only been this afternoon. "You made me stay behind."

"And I haven't thanked you for doing as I asked. I know it was hard for you to sit and wait."

"You have no idea."

"But it was difficult enough sneaking in alone. It would have been too risky to—"

"I understand."

"You do, don't you?" He stopped walking and turned to her. "Why do I sense this underlying sadness in you? Are you okay? Was there a problem at the police station?"

She shook her head. "I'm just tired." And he was on top of the world. Exhilarated. Which simply made her realize how far apart their worlds really were and always would be.

"It's more than fatigue," he insisted.

When had he gotten to know her so well? She didn't want to talk about her feelings for him. Not when she still felt so unsettled. She'd only realized that she loved him in the last few hours and had yet

to explore all the ramifications of what those emotions implied.

"I never knew that just sitting and waiting could be so stressful. If you'd been caught..."

"I wasn't."

She tried to continue walking, but he gently gripped her arm, impeding her progress. Grateful that he couldn't read the expression in her eyes, she suppressed her doubts about continuing her fling. She didn't like hiding her love, didn't want to burden him with the truth. She just wanted to have a good time on her vacation with him and then go home to lick her wounds.

But she wasn't good at fooling herself. Now that she knew that she loved him, everything had changed. She couldn't go on pretending that wonderful sex and a charming companion were enough to make her content. She'd never been interested in short-term relationships.

His voice rough, rousing and ready to challenge her, demanded, "Talk to me."

"About what?" she countered.

"What's going on in your head?"

"I was just thinking about those files Logan Kincaid sent," she lied.

"Yeah, right."

"How could he do extensive research so quickly? I saw them flash on the screen before you printed them. Those files were long, went back years and covered everything from credit card debts to phone bills to schools attended."

"It's going to eat away at you until you open up."

Obviously he wasn't buying her attempt to distract him. Frustration added an edge to her tone. "Did you ever think I might not want to share every thought in my head with you?"

"No."

She snorted. "Then maybe you should think again."

"Fine."

"Fine."

They began to stroll again, but she'd taken back her hand and they no longer touched. While this wasn't their first argument, she suspected it might be the beginning of the end of their relationship and melancholy gripped her. So much for a carefree fling. So much for letting herself enjoy a breezy vacation with a good-looking hunk. Except she'd never been able to look at any man that way—never mind Jason. Sex came connected not just to a hot body but to a real live person—a person with feelings and worries and goals, and she suspected her mood had put a damper on his successful mission.

She didn't want to spoil his exhilaration and yet, as much as she tried, she couldn't quite hide her sadness.

He glanced sideways at her. "You do understand that I don't have a clue what's wrong here?"

"Uh-huh."

"And that I can't read your mind?"

"Uh-huh."

Abruptly, he changed the subject. "A woman was driving down a road in the opposite direction to a man behind the wheel of his own car. She rolled down her

window and yelled 'Pig.' He yelled back, 'Bitch,' and kept driving. Around the next curve, his car struck a pig that had wandered into the road. And the moral of that story is..."

"Men are aggressive?" she guessed, suspecting he was pressing her again, but couldn't figure out where he was going with this.

"Men need to listen. Well, I'm listening, babe, but you aren't talking."

Kimberly had never felt less like talking in her life. If she was as daring as Maggie, she'd lure Jason into bed, distract him from a conversation she wasn't ready to have. But she couldn't think about making love right now. She needed to give her emotions time to settle and to come to grips with her feelings.

"I really am tired." She knew he didn't believe her, but all she wanted to do was rush up to her room, take a long hot bath and then sleep. She didn't want to think about him and her for the next twelve hours.

When they approached the hotel, cop cars were just leaving. They entered through the front door and Jason spoke to the kid behind the desk. "What's going on?"

"The police said that someone stole a diamond from the museum. On a hot tip, they searched a bunch of our rooms, including yours, but found nothing. And then they heard that the diamond was back at the museum after all, so they left. Odd, huh?"

"Very." Jason walked her to her room without saying another word. When he followed her into her room, she wanted to demand that he leave, but that would require explaining and she simply didn't have

the energy. She left him in her room with her laptop and his files from Logan Kincaid while she ran a bath.

No sooner had she settled into the hot water than he strolled inside the bathroom, closed the lid of the commode and sat on the throne with her laptop balanced on his knees. "Our fellow travelers have more than their share of secrets hidden in their pasts."

She lathered a washcloth with soap and smoothed it over her skin. She'd thought to bathe in privacy and silence, but his statement had provoked her curiosity. "Like what?"

"Alex, surfer boy, has a record."

"Really?"

"As a juvie, he stole a goat."

"A goat?"

"Probably a school mascot, but after junior high school, the nature of his crimes altered in severity. Breaking and entering. Car theft. He sold drugs in college."

"With that record, how did he get accepted to college?" She leaned her head back and let the hot water take the strain from her muscles.

"His father made a large donation to the university. The newest wing of the medical school bears their name."

"Okay. What else?"

"The Barrs have been married and divorced four times—"

She frowned. "But this trip is to celebrate their twentieth anniversary."

"They've been married and divorced four times to

one another. I guess they count anniversaries from their first wedding.'' He hit a few keys and moved on.

She shrugged, and used her toe to turn on the tap to add more hot water. The trickling sound relaxed her as much as the heat did. ''Anything on our astrologer?''

''Caroline? She's been in and out of several mental institutions.''

''Any violent tendencies?'' she asked.

''None.''

''And the professor and his trophy wife?''

''She has a record. Used to be a hooker.''

Kimberly's eyes popped wide open. ''You're kidding!''

Jason shook his head and stared at his screen. ''Oh, this is interesting. The professor teaches screenwriting at the University of Orlando in Florida. You ever enter your script in a contest there?''

''No.'' She sat up so fast that water splashed in the tub.

''What?'' Jason might have kept his thoughts on track but his gaze focused on her breasts.

She eased back under the water, trying to make her action casual, but he had to have noticed that at his look her nipples had tightened to hard nubs. But she wasn't cold and had to use her toes to turn off the hot water spigot. ''We do send scripts to what we call a first reader in Orlando. As head of the department, Professor Jamison might know him.''

''And?''

''Maybe I'm overly sensitive, but the professor has made a few jealous comments.'' She fought with her-

self not to cover her breasts. She wasn't cold, but maybe he'd think she was, instead of responding to the appreciation in his gaze. "But I can't picture the professor stealing the *Book of Celts* or the Star of the North and even if he could, what would be his motive?"

"Jealousy? Theft of your idea? Revenge?"

"Now you're really reaching."

His eyes brightened. "What I'd like to reach for…is your heart."

Oh, God. Why did he have to say the very thing that made her feel as though she was shattering into pieces? Her chest tightened and she had difficulty speaking around the lump in her throat. Was he saying he wanted her to have feelings for him? Because maybe he had them for her. "My heart?"

"Yes. I wish I could massage it. Warm it up. Keep it safe."

The burning heat in his eyes seared her.

She licked her bottom lip nervously. Damn, the man didn't play fair. He'd allowed her to feel safe and pampered in her hot bath. Then he'd switched the conversation from business to personal so fast that he'd spiked her desire when she hadn't even been thinking about lovemaking. He shouldn't turn on practical Kimberly with his sexy looks, but he did. So how had Jason managed to make her feel sexy and wanton and desirable when she was tired and hadn't even had sex on her mind? It was if he'd flipped a switch, a switch that only he knew existed. And she could no longer recall exactly why making love to him again was a bad idea.

She lathered the washcloth, slowly and deliberately. And this time, she removed one leg from the water, pointed her toe at the ceiling and made a production of allowing the suds to run down her leg in thick soapy trickles while she washed the arch of her foot, her ankle, her calf and her thigh.

He sucked in a breath when she repeated the maneuver with her other leg. This time, she knew if he climbed into the tub with her that she'd be on the receiving end of a lot more than a foot massage.

So she had to bite back disappointment when his gaze returned to the laptop's screen. "Professor Jamison has no criminal record. He lives in a four-bedroom home by the college campus and has two adult children from a former marriage."

"He sounds boring."

"Those are always the ones you have to watch." His eyes twinkled as he watched her lather her breasts. "How many times have you seen neighbors in the news interviewed saying, 'He was so quiet and kept to himself.'"

She held the washcloth over her breasts and wrung it out, allowing the water to wash away the soap. He watched her every move, then his blue eyes returned to the computer. Damn him.

What did he want? An invitation?

She knew what she wanted, one last time together with this man she loved. One final night in his arms before she said goodbye.

"Logan Kincaid just e-mailed me. The Shey Group has conclusive evidence that the professor had direct access to your script. According to their analysis,

there's a probability of over ninety-eight percent that he's the thief.''

''That's just a theory and will do us no good unless we can catch the bastard.'' Then she changed her tone to deliberately low. Husky. Provocative. ''Aren't you going to join me?''

''I'm not sure.'' He turned those twinkling blue eyes on her, and she could see mischief layered with desire. ''But I think better in a hot bathtub.''

She arched her eyebrow, her heart hammering her ribs. ''Is thinking all that you can do in a bathtub?''

''Oh, I might come up…with…other interesting possibilities.''

''If I shared this tub with you, would you be willing to wash my back?''

''Darling, you let me share that tub with you and I'll not only wash you, I'll lick the excess water off you…with my tongue.''

Despite the heat of the hot water, despite the sad lump in her throat that this would be their last time together, a shiver of anticipation licked down her spine and curled in her stomach. ''Take off your clothes.''

''In any particular order?''

''Your shirt.''

She leaned back as he ripped off his shirt and tossed it over the sink. Muscles rippled across his powerful chest dusted with swirls of dark hair that narrowed about his flat stomach. She liked looking at him and took her time, allowing her gaze to appreciate the hard, lean length of him.

He placed his hands on his hips, a cocky smile

curling one side of his mouth and emphasizing the gleam in his eyes. He looked every inch a dangerous jewel thief about to snatch a precious diamond and make it his own.

"Now the rest." She gestured to his leather pants, expecting to enjoy the sight of him wriggling out of them. But the material had a hook-and-loop fastener, and he stripped them off along with his shorts in one graceful move that left her breathless.

He stepped into the tub. "Scoot up."

She'd thought he'd sit by her feet but instead he sat behind her, his long legs surrounding hers, his chest brushing her back, his head dipping to allow his lips to nip her earlobe.

She tossed him the washcloth. "Hey, you promised to wash my back."

"I promised you a lot more than that." His tone, seductive and sultry, matched the warmth of his hands. Ignoring the washcloth, he plucked the soap from the dish, lathered his hands and then slicked them over her shoulders. His fingers found knotted muscles and released them.

She'd never known she could be so relaxed and so excited at the same time. He caressed her back with steady strokes, but all the while his breath fanned her ear, and occasionally he planted a kiss on her shoulder or neck.

And as good as her back and shoulders felt, she was eager to turn around. Her breasts already ached for the touch of his hands and his mouth, her lips for his kiss. And she yearned to run her palms over his chest, to his flat stomach and deeper, between his

legs. Sitting still became difficult, so she placed her palms on his hard thighs and started making small, circular stokes up and down the insides of his legs with her palms.

"Impatient wench."

She giggled. "Have you heard me complaining?"

"You have your own way of talking and I heard you loud and clear." His jutting erection pressed against the small of her back. "However, I promised to wash all of you and I intend to do just that."

"Okay. But I get to reciprocate."

When he again reached for the soap she thought he would finally reach around for her breasts. But instead, he murmured, "Tuck your knees under you and kneel."

She did as he asked coming up out of the water. He washed her lower back and bottom as thoroughly as he'd done her shoulders, leaving not one inch of flesh untouched. Although she parted her knees, he didn't once graze his fingers between her thighs.

When he began to work his way down her legs, she muttered, "I already washed them."

"But I didn't."

When he reached the spot behind her knees, she giggled. "That tickles. And I'm getting cold."

"Where?"

"My breasts."

"Hmm. I suppose my hands could warm them up."

Finally, he was going to touch her. But no, not yet. Instead he began at her knees, sliding his hands over her upper thighs, and then guiding her hips back down into the water so her folded legs under her kept her thighs open and ready for him.

But he seemed in no rush at all, skipping her mons to her belly where he seemed to spend an inordinate amount of time before giving attention to her rib cage, swirling his soapy fingers over her belly button and tummy and hips. Her breasts, swelling with need, had never felt so sensitive. And he had yet to touch her there.

"What would you like most right now?" he asked.

"To feel you inside me."

"That's not going to happen for a while."

"Why not?"

"Because waiting makes you more sensitive."

"Waiting makes me more impatient. I don't want to wait."

"I know. But you will do this for me, yes?" He cupped her breasts from underneath, lifting her and flicking his thumbs over her nipples, shooting heat straight to her core. "Now, aren't I worth waiting for?"

"Yes, but…"

"But what?"

"Now I want you even more."

"That was the idea." He chuckled, rounding his palms over her breasts, teasing, stroking, plucking.

"Your ideas are…not…so…bad."

He nibbled the back of her neck. "I'm glad you approve. Are you still cold?"

"A little."

"Why don't you lean forward and turn on a trickle of hot water."

She did as he asked, then his fingers slid from her breasts to between her thighs, parting her folds and

she gasped with the pleasure of him finding her there. "You planned that, didn't you?"

"Mmm."

She rested on her hands and knees, her breasts in the warm water, his hand creating a fire of need between her legs. "I can't—"

"Are you uncomfy?"

"No, but—"

"You can do anything you want. Don't you feel good?"

He was driving her wild, his finger dipping inside her heat while at the same time he rubbed her clit, yet never giving enough pressure for release. "I need more."

"Of course you do." But he kept right on doing what he was doing. His fingers playing and plucking but never quite finishing what they started.

"I want you inside me."

"Okay."

He agreed but didn't so much as change his position one centimeter and she groaned in protest.

"Now would be good."

"You think?"

"Please." To her own ears, her voice sounded wanton and desperate.

"Soon. First I'm going to rinse all the soap off you and then I'm going to follow through on the rest of my promise."

She had no idea what he was talking about. Her body clenched with unspilled tension. She was about to claw at him. Ready to explode.

And then he pulled his hands away, depriving her of his touch, depriving her of release.

"I promised to lick you dry. Remember?"

13

"LATER. You can dry me later." Kimberly demanded and Jason loved making her wild, loved drawing her out of her practical self, loved revealing her passionate nature.

"Such impatience," he teased, but in actuality holding back with her had caused his muscles to strain, his heartbeat to increase to thudding levels and his erection, to stiffen. He'd never been this ready to explode or this ready to tamp down his own needs in order to give them both more pleasure.

Part of him craved the ultimate satisfaction of driving into her heat. Yet another part of him wanted to see exactly how far they could go together, not just physically, but mentally and emotionally. He certainly hadn't expected her to make him feel happy enough to consider making important changes in his life in order to stay with her, but he was ready to do whatever it took to keep her. She'd captivated his interest and captured his heart.

He slipped on a condom, then rubbed his erection between her legs. She rocked back and forth, open and ready to receive him deep inside her, but instead, he stroked against her slick warmth, while his fingers played slip and slide with her clit.

She panted, rocking her hips, wild to take him inside her. With any other woman he would have taken his own pleasure by now. But with Kimberly, he loved seeing her wanting him so much that she forgot to hide behind her shell.

Right now there were no barriers between them. Just bare flesh. Primitive and raw needs. And more enjoyment that he'd ever conceived possible.

He didn't know exactly the moment when her pleasure had become more important than his own, but he recognized that he'd never felt this way about a woman. Kimberly was special. Different. Precious.

Before he lost control and took what he wanted so desperately, he tossed a towel on the floor next to the tub and then helped her out of the water. Her face flushed from the heat, had a reckless gleam in her eyes.

Her lips were full and pouty. "You've tortured me long enough. I believe it's *my* turn."

She leaned over, placed those lush lips around his nipple. And bit him. The sharp nip followed by her lapping tongue was a systematic pattern of pain and pleasure that she inflicted on both nipples, his neck and his buttocks.

She seemed to know exactly where he was sensitive and she focused on those areas with a healthy glint of challenge in her eyes. He stood perfectly still, allowing her to have her way with him, enjoying both her attention and her pleasure at arousing him beyond what he'd thought were his limits.

Kimberly didn't seem to recognize limits. Now set

free, her boundless enthusiasm soared, taking him to a place where thinking became difficult.

When she cupped his balls, his first inclination was to lean into her touch, but he forced his feet to root into the floor, letting her explore at will. But when his breath came in short, painful gasps, when he told himself he could take only another minute and then another minute more, when he feared he'd lose control, he tried to sweep her into his arms.

"No." She squeezed his balls, demanding that he hold still, taking charge. "You made me wait. It's time you had some of your own medicine."

He could barely believe her brazen command and he found that he enjoyed this side of her, too. But her caresses were driving him wild. "Now, Kimberly—"

"Don't you 'now Kimberly' me. It's my turn to play. Your turn to wait."

And he did. Sweat popped out on his scalp, his breath came in ragged gasps. He must have clenched and unclenched his fists a dozen times. Until he burned. Until he knew he would explode. Until he let out a roar of frustration and finally swept her into his arms and carried her toward the bed.

He'd meant to lick her dry, but he couldn't wait another second. He needed to take her now.

They never made it to the bed. Somehow, she wrapped her long legs around him and they ended up on their sides, face-to-face, on the rug.

"I'm sorry," he murmured in her ear.

"For giving me the best sex of my life?" She shifted so she was on top of him.

"I can't wait."

"I can't, either." And she took him into her heat. But that wasn't enough. She slanted her mouth over his, taking, demanding as she gyrated her hips, riding him, setting a pace that took his breath. When he reached for her breasts, she grabbed his wrists, held them by his head. Then she rode him hard.

He couldn't close his eyes. Couldn't get enough of watching her expressive face. The green fire in her eyes, the bold set of her jaw, the determined angle of her chin.

She was magnificent in her passion, this wild, wanton woman who was taking him to a place he'd never been. All the blood in his body seemed to have gone south. His head was spinning, his thoughts dizzy from lack of oxygen. And all the spiraling tension focused deep in his center and blossomed under her expert gyrations, mushrooming into a swell of epic need.

And then she ceased all movement. Held perfectly still.

Through a cloud of confusion, he growled. She'd brought him right to the edge, he was dangling by a frayed thread. "What's wrong?"

"Nothing." She smiled at him, a wide, pleased-with-herself smile that would have taken his breath away if he'd had any air left in his lungs.

"Why...did...you...stop?"

"Because."

What the hell was she saying? He couldn't think through the haze of desire she'd woven around them. And then as the raging lust abated just a little, he realized she'd turned the tables on him. Taken him

right to the brink of orgasm, then left him frustrated and unbalanced. Almost desperate.

That's when he knew he was going to fulfill his promise to her—even if it killed him. Inch by inch, he would lick every centimeter of her dry.

Without saying one word, he rolled them over. Remaining inside her for now, he began with her ear, lapping off the water droplets suckling her cute little earlobe. And when she squirmed under him and let out a breathy sigh, his determination to wait longer hardened.

When he abandoned that ear for the other one, then moved down her neck, her hips tried to pump against his. But he held her immobile with his weight, pinning her to the floor, denying them both what they wanted.

Her head tossed from side to side. "Surely you aren't..."

"I am."

"But—"

"You reminded me of my promise, and now I intend to keep it."

As his tongue licked her breast, she wiggled and groaned. "Please. Can't we finish?"

"Sure. You go right ahead."

But she wouldn't come. Not unless he touched the right places, and he wasn't inclined to do so any time soon. Not after the little minx had taken him all the way to within a nanosecond of orgasm and then backed down.

He kept his hips still, enjoying her soft moan of pleasure and her hands attempting to urge his hips to

move. He especially liked the way her breath rasped and her fingers dug into his back.

He lapped at the hollow at her hip, the shadow of her belly button, plunging ever downward until his sex eased from her warmth. But he needed a break from her heat, needed to control his own undeniable urges.

And then his mouth hovered over her mons and he parted her legs. She tasted like nectar from the gods, sweet and musky. When his mouth came down over her and his tongue swirled over her clit, her hands dug into his hair, her back arched, and funny little coos emerged from the back of her throat.

"I'm…going…to…"

"Ah, please…"

"Yes."

He sensed her trembling, clenching, tightening. Just a little more would shoot her out of control. And that's when he stopped, rolled her on top again.

"Take me, Kimberly, darling. Take everything you want."

And she did. Her hips bucked and thrust. There was no going back this time. Her eyes closed, her face raw and needy, she clenched around him, taking him deep and then she was spasming around him, taking him with her. Exploding.

He didn't recall her collapsing on top of him. But then he'd lost it for a few seconds or a full minute there. But now he cradled her against his chest, ran his hands through her hair and felt like the luckiest man alive.

"You were wonderful."

She snuggled closer. "So were you. I've never felt that good."

They *were* good together and he didn't mean just sexually. He enjoyed her company. He looked forward to holding her, to waking up next to her, looked forward to being part of her life. Vowing to make it happen, he tugged the sheet from the bed over them, perfectly content to be her pillow until morning. It was his last coherent thought before he drifted off to sleep.

KIMBERLY SEARCHED through the extensive files Logan Kincaid had sent, especially the one on the professor. She found nothing out of the ordinary and was about to shut down her computer when she came across one last file, marked Omega.

She clicked open the file. A short one-pager. The CIA had concluded that her parents' deaths were accidental. The theory was they'd been sucked down by a strong current, become lost in the underwater cave and had taken too long to surface, creating an excruciating condition called the bends. Preferring fast deaths to long and painful ones, her parents had chosen not to suffer. Hence the poison in their bloodstreams.

Her parents had died as they'd lived. Together.

Tears streamed down her cheeks as she read how their bodies had been found in an embrace. And now they were together for all eternity.

Kimberly swallowed the lump in her throat. Knowing the truth was better than eternally wondering. And

she felt a tension easing in her heart that she hadn't known existed.

Thanks to Logan Kincaid and Jason Parker she had a sense of relief and had a place she'd never been able to go. She would always miss her parents, but the love they'd given her would stay with her forever.

"What's wrong?" Jason asked, shoving aside the sheets and padding over from the bed in his bare feet. He placed a comforting hand on her shoulder.

She turned the laptop screen so he could read it. "I'm okay. And thank Logan Kincaid for me."

After reading the file, he drew her into his arms and held her, giving her comfort as well as time to regroup to set her thoughts in order. Today was not about the past. Her problems weren't connected to her parents, but were all her own.

For the moment, she liked snuggling against Jason, enjoyed the strength of his arms around her. More importantly, she appreciated that he cherished holding her just to hold her.

The man really was perfect for her—except they came from different worlds. She lived in one place, Los Angeles. California was the epicenter of the movie industry. His work took him to every continent, barring Antarctica. Her life was safe, practical. His life was always at risk. They had no future together, but being with him felt so right.

She shoved away the sadness of the past and the pain she'd feel without him in her future for the pragmatic matters in the present. "I wish we could bring in the police on what is going on—"

"They'd arrest us. Besides, I can't go to the authorities," he reminded her gently.

She sat on the sofa, drawing her knees to her chest. "Of course you can't. I'm sorry. The news about my parents must have—"

"It's okay." He poured coffee that she'd fixed earlier and handed her a mug.

She sipped, appreciated the kick of caffeine. "So what do we do next?"

"Eat. Rest. Follow the script. And then we do what you suggested, come up with a plan to catch the culprit."

She thought back to her story. "We're heading to Edinburgh, Scotland, next."

"The problem is that we don't know exactly what the stalker plans to do next. Whoever stole the *Book of Celts* after you left the library must have stashed the book outside their hotel room, since the police searched all of our rooms and didn't find it."

Jason paced and drank his coffee and she couldn't help admiring his bare chest and powerful shoulders. She liked the way he looked in the morning with his flyaway black hair and his pajama bottoms just barely clinging to his narrow hips. She wouldn't mind waking up to the sight of him every day. Her heart skipped and she told it to settle down.

Jason continued to pace. "While he's a man of superior taste in jewels, it makes setting a trap more difficult because we don't know what he's after."

Kimberly snapped her fingers, an idea forming. "Wait a minute. The missing script from the printer

only has the version I wrote *before* Quinn requested his revisions.''

Jason eyed her over the brim of his coffee cup. "How will that help?"

"Quinn didn't change any of the suspense elements. Only asked me to add the love scenes. If we have a conversation about Quinn's changes, but aren't too specific, then no one can anticipate our moves. They won't know that Quinn didn't change the suspense. Since we won't be following the script, it'll force whoever is doing this to come after us."

Jason nodded in agreement. "We should allow the entire tour group to overhear us. And, I'm going to call Logan for more help from his team. While we set up this trap, I want the tour members tailed and taped—so we have more than our word as evidence."

She grinned at him. "This could work out. If I have a tape of someone doing something illegal, you needn't be involved with the authorities at all."

"You have a knack for plotting. Are you sure you wouldn't like to become a jewel thief?" he teased.

"You must be kidding. With all this material, I have enough research for my next three scripts."

"Oh, I don't think so." Jason put aside his coffee cup, a glint she recognized in his eyes.

However, she played dumb to egg him on. "What do you mean?"

"I don't believe you've done enough research for your love scenes."

Perhaps it wasn't quite time to say goodbye. Would her heart hurt any less later if they made love a few more times before she had to return to the States

alone? Kimberly fought to keep her voice steady. "You know, I believe you're correct. I should research making love first thing in the morning."

"Absolutely," he agreed.

"In a Welsh hotel room."

"Want to try the bed?"

"Beds are boring."

"Is that a challenge?" He reached for her and she scooted around the couch.

"Maybe. First, you have to catch me."

When he moved around the couch, she raced toward the balcony. She never made it. His long legs narrowed the distance between them in seconds.

He clasped her wrist, tugged her to him, then using one of his hands, he held both her wrists behind her back, capturing her, keeping her exactly where she wanted to be.

She tossed her hair back. "Well, now you've caught me. What are you going to do about it?"

His hand closed over her breast and she gasped, looked down and then chuckled. He'd unbuttoned her blouse again—without her feeling a thing. However, she sure was feeling his hand now. Her breast tingled beneath his hand, responding immediately to his touch.

So much for resting, eating or planning. She much preferred making love.

Lifting her chin, she locked gazes with those mesmerizing blue eyes of his. "So, is that the best you can do?"

"THE QUEEN'S CROWN is the next item on my list," Kimberly told Caroline and Alex, who sat in train

seats opposite them. However, she spoke loudly enough for the professor and his wife, in the seats behind them, to hear, as well as the Barrs across the aisle.

Liam eyed her with interest. "Edinburgh is an elegant city of marvelous architecture that sits among rolling hills and ancient volcanoes."

The professor's wife sighed. "Enough with the tour guide stuff. Liam, tell us about the Queen's Crown, please."

Beside his wife the professor rolled his eyes. "You should have read up before the trip. Or I could have—"

"Please, Liam," his wife interrupted her husband, a habit that caused the professor to frown. "Isn't there some famous love story connected to that crown?"

Their guide smiled. "It's more of a legend than history."

"It's pure fairy tale," the professor muttered in exasperation.

Beside Kimberly, Jason sat reading a newspaper, seemingly paying no attention to the conversation. But Kimberly knew better.

Jason was always at his most dangerous when he was misdirecting other people, preventing them from noticing exactly what he was doing. He worked much like a magician, using distraction as his secret weapon.

He'd had her off balance and distracted since the moment they'd met. Even when she thought she knew her own mind, he had a way of altering her opinions to coincide with his own. She hadn't intended to make

love with him again. Why dig into a deeper emotional hole when it would only make climbing out more difficult? And yet, making love to him had been simply irresistible.

She wished she could talk to Maggie. Or Cate. Both of her friends were strong, independent women who would help her to see why she couldn't seem ever to say no to Jason. Just because she loved the man didn't mean all her self-protective instincts had been left behind in the United States. And yet, she'd never been in love before. She and Jason felt right together.

She glanced at Jason. At first look, he appeared calm. He sat slightly slouched in his seat with his long legs stretched into the aisle, his ankles crossed. He held the newspaper before him, but his eyes didn't sweep back and forth as if he was reading, and she suspected he was covertly watching their fellow travelers.

Liam began his story and Kimberly leaned her head against Jason's shoulder as she listened to the guide's deep voice. ''Benbrochie Castle was built by Black Angus McEwan in the thirteenth century. A strong and respected laird who guarded the border with a ferocious strength and the power of his sword arm, he needed sons to help protect the vast lands he'd won during the previous war.''

''Can you skip the war part and just get to the love story?'' Trixie requested.

''If that's all right with the gentlemen?'' Liam asked.

At the nods of agreement, he went on, "Black Angus's first wife died in childbirth along with the babe. His second wife took ill with the pox before she quickened with child. And his third wife threw herself off the rampart two weeks after the wedding. Legend has it that Black Angus wore her out in the bedroom, so desperate was the man to have sons."

Kimberly wondered if that part of the legend was true. Obviously Black Angus didn't have Jason's bedroom skills. Her body still tingled from his earlier lovemaking. If they'd been alone, she would have been more than ready for another round right now.

Sitting snuggled against him, her thigh pressed to his had its own kind of stimulation. She recalled the strength of the muscles in those legs, the light dusting of hair, the cords that barely strained when he...

She had to stop daydreaming like a teenage girl.

Listen to the story.

Watch your fellow travelers. Were any of them overly interested?

"Deciding that ladies weren't hardy enough for breeding, Black Angus wed the peasant girl, Morven. She gave him five sons and he was so pleased with her that he commissioned the Queen's Crown. Although Morven wasn't a queen, he was determined to treat her like one."

"That's so romantic," Mrs. Barr sighed.

"Not exactly," Liam told her. "Morven had a roving eye and when Black Angus caught her in the stable with a groom, he banished her from Argyle Castle, and she supposedly spent the rest of her life begging for alms. In truth, she probably became a prostitute.

Black Angus kept the Queen's Crown to remind him that no wife could be trusted. He never remarried. His oldest son took his lands away from him in a bloody war that lasted a decade and pitted brother against brother. It was rumored that the crown was cursed. Any woman who wore it would be unfaithful.''

"How is the crown connected to your movie?" Caroline asked Kimberly.

She didn't bother explaining that her story was not yet a movie, but a screenplay. "My dying spy left a microchip on the crown, knowing that only the most skilled thief could recover the information."

Trixie clapped her hands together. "Clever."

The professor glared at her.

Alex rolled his eyes and Caroline sighed. "I'll have to see if I can do a star chart on Black Angus and Morven. Obviously their marriage was ill-fated and poorly timed. Do we know their birthdays?"

Liam shook his head. "I would recommend that you all spend your first day at Edinburgh Castle and walk the Royal Mile, a historical…"

Kimberly let him go on telling them about the city. When he finished, she kept her tone casual. "We want to see Edinburgh Castle, too. But first, we're going to Argyle Castle. The crown is not only a legend. It's very valuable."

"Really?" Alex asked.

Kimberly didn't have to force enthusiasm into her voice. "The diamonds, rubies and pearls are merely a backdrop for the prized emerald."

Jason finally made his contribution to the conver-

sation. "The center stone is supposed to be as big as Morven's right breast."

His statement caught everyone's attention.

"Just her right breast?" Alex asked. "Now that's weird."

"I have never heard that interpretation," the professor commented. "Would you mind telling us your source?"

The professor clearly wanted to challenge Jason's knowledge. Who would ever remember the source of that kind of information?

However, Jason didn't so much as bat one eyelash. "The *International Guide to Royal Jewels and Gemstones.*"

While the group went on talking about comparing a stone size to a breast, Kimberly grinned and whispered to Jason. "You sure put the professor in his place."

"I couldn't resist."

She recognized that mischievous tone. "What?"

"There's no such thing as the *International Guide to Royal Jewels and Gemstones.* I made it up."

"All of it?"

"I have nipples on the brain lately. Your fault."

Kimberly choked back a laugh. Jason was clearly enjoying himself and so was she. But the train ride into Edinburgh would end all too soon. Then they would be setting their trap and her nerves would string taut.

Although Jason had made his request to Logan Kincaid last night about another member of the Shey Group joining them to secretly tape their journey, Lo-

gan couldn't guarantee the man's arrival in time. Something about a no-fly zone due to bad weather in Africa. The pilot, Jack Donovan, had promised to do his best to deliver L.J. to back them up, and Logan had assured him that if Jack wouldn't fly, it wasn't doable.

Which, for now, meant that they were on their own. Jason had yet to hear from the pilot or his mysterious passenger, L.J., a man so well respected that he could turn over the tape to the British authorities and the tape's veracity would be accepted—no questions asked.

Now all they had to do was hope that someone took the bait.

14

JASON HADN'T KNOWN Kimberly long enough to know if she was a moody person. However, since yesterday, she'd seemed a little down. And he didn't understand it. He'd tried and failed to get her to talk to him. They'd made love. And they had probably figured out who was framing her. Now all they had to do was catch the professor. She had every reason to be up and excited but clearly she wasn't.

He didn't like *not* knowing what was going on in that head of hers. He didn't like that she wouldn't talk to him about it. Obviously, she trusted him enough to make love, but not enough to share all of her problems. Trust took time. He understood that and he was trying to be patient.

The distraction of traveling with the rest of the group and planning how to catch the person who had tried to frame her had helped to take his mind off more personal problems. Once they exited the train and headed toward Benbrochie Castle, he would slip into mission mode where he focused solely on successfully evading the authorities while carrying out their scheme.

Which didn't mean his frustration would end. He'd never connected with another woman as he had with Kimberly. Usually after a lusty tumble or two in bed,

his interest in a lady waned and he moved on. But with Kimberly, he wanted her more now than he had before the first time they'd made love.

He wished he could extend her vacation into a six-month tour of the continent. But their journey together would be over in just a few more days and saying a permanent goodbye didn't sit well with him. However, with the train pulling into Waverley Station, he couldn't dwell on the future.

They gathered their bags and Liam had a taxi lined up to haul the luggage ahead to the hotel. Meanwhile, he and Kimberly grabbed another cab and headed straight to Benbrochie Castle.

The moment they entered the taxi, Jason's cell phone rang. "Hello?"

"I've got your six."

Logan's pilot had delivered L.J. who would be watching their backs. "Excellent. We appreciate the help."

Jason placed an arm over Kimberly's shoulders. She peered out the window with interest at the intersection of Market and Princess streets. He had been to the city many times before and enjoyed watching her eyes widening at the beauty of Waverley Bridge and her appreciation of the stone facades and the towering walls of the Old Town.

"We're all set?" she asked him.

"Yeah. Kincaid runs an efficient organization." Jason was impressed. The Shey Group had delivered information and backup as promised. Jason hadn't been part of a team since his stint in the military, but he enjoyed working with other competent people.

While he didn't like endangering Kimberly, he

didn't think there was much likelihood of danger. And with L.J. watching out for them, the mission should go down just the way they'd planned.

But Jason had been in business too long and had been too successful not to plan for contingencies. "If anything should go wrong, I want you to contact Logan Kincaid at the number I gave you."

At his words, Kimberly turned from the window and looked at him. "Are you having second thoughts?"

"I'm just careful."

"You sure?"

"Yes." He stroked her bare shoulder. She was wearing shorts, a tight sleeveless tank top and sneakers and was toting a purse. With the camera around her neck and the sunglasses perched on her head, she looked the typical American tourist.

She was young and eager and stepped out of the cab with an exuberance he wished he could match. As he'd instructed, she didn't look around for the professor, just took in the sights.

Jason didn't spot L.J., but he didn't expect to—especially since he had no idea what the man looked like. He bought tickets in the square outside that was full of vendors selling souvenirs, and then they entered the castle, walking over a bridge that spanned a moat that must have once been filled with water but was now all grass.

With the castle's stone walls casting shadows, the temperature dropped. Goose bumps rose on Kimberly's arms, but she didn't complain. She was too busy looking at the polished silver armor. Guarding the entrance doors stood a six-foot-tall knight in full

regalia. Beside him, a massive wooden horse with a heavy saddle showed how the animal was protected during battle.

Jason checked his watch. "We have time to wander around a bit but—"

"—you want to check out the Queen's Crown first," she finished his sentence for him. "So we have an escape route?"

"You know me too well," he muttered, wondering if he was getting predictable, stale. In truth, stealing stones had begun to lose its glamour several years ago. Recently, he'd taken only enough jobs to keep his customers happy and his skills up-to-date.

But sharing the experience with Kimberly and seeing it anew in her eyes made him realize how much he loved every part of the job. Intense research. The challenge of fencing the stones. Setting a price. And of course the actual heist.

The only comparable experience that gave him as much pleasure as practicing his craft…was making love with Kimberly. He wished they had time for a little afternoon delight, but he wanted to give whoever was pursuing them every opportunity to spot them and follow.

When Alex and Caroline turned a corner and practically bumped into Jason and Kimberly, Kimberly greeted them warmly. "Glad to see you two made it."

"We just saw the Queen's Crown," Caroline jerked her thumb over her shoulder. "She must have had a neck ache after carrying all that weight on her head."

Jason believed he'd just seen the professor and his wife skulking down the hall and displayed some of his knowledge to make conversation. "That's why in modern times the crowns became more delicate, the gold and silver less elaborate and the stones smaller in size."

Alex tugged on Caroline's arm. "Well we're off to walk the Royal Mile, and then we hope to take a bus tour around the city. I hear the place is known for good architecture."

Caroline dug her elbow into Alex's ribs. "You just want to make out on the top of the double-decker."

After they left, Kimberly kept her voice low. "Did it seem to you that Alex went out of his way to claim they were leaving the castle?"

"He could have meant it. I just saw the professor and Trixie head toward the room with the Queen's Crown."

"You still want to go that way?" Kimberly stopped to admire a twelfth-century exhibit of a peasant's outfit.

"Why not?"

They hadn't reached the room that kept a good portion of the Scottish Jewel Collection when they heard glass breaking. Then three gunshots. Lots of screaming.

"Something went wrong." Jason yanked Kimberly out of the way of a mob of frantic people dashing past them toward the exits.

Kimberly tugged him toward the door, too. "Let's go."

"You go ahead. I need to find out what happened."

"No, you don't." Kimberly followed the crowd of fleeing tourists, tugging him toward the exit, her strength surprisingly fierce. "You aren't even armed."

Jason hesitated whether to break Kimberly's grip on his arm. Torn between making sure she got safely out of the building or checking to see what had happened, he peered over his shoulder. However, as important as completing his mission was to him, her safety came first.

"Fine. We'll go together."

"Good."

"But you may be giving up the chance to clear your name."

An alarm sounded and more people rushed by. They bumped into another couple fleeing the building. And the smoke from the gunshots left a bitter bite in the air.

Jason hoped the cops would arrive in time to catch the culprit. It was odd thinking of law enforcement as helpful, but his take on things had altered since he'd met Kimberly. But she was worth it.

Just then the professor charged around the corner with the Queen's Crown in his hand. Jason hadn't thought the old guy could move that fast. His eyes glimmered with triumph as he spied Jason and Kimberly and pounded straight for them.

When the professor flung the heavy crown at Kimberly's head, Jason snagged it, his protective action instinctive. A moment later the police stormed into the room, and he still held the incriminating crown. In the confusion, Jason doubted anyone had witnessed what had really happened.

KIMBERLY PACED in a jail cell, furious that nothing had gone as they'd planned. And she was worried sick about Jason, whom she hadn't seen since the police had carted him off in a separate vehicle. She fought back the fear, not for herself, but for Jason, who had been holding the Queen's Crown when the police had arrived.

Because he'd agreed to help her, Jason was now under lock and key. If the authorities learned about his past, he might never see the other side of the jail cell again.

Damn the professor. He'd meant for *her* to catch the crown—so the police would think her guilty. Only, Jason had been too quick, saving her from injury, but taking the blame onto his own broad shoulders.

Oh God. He could spend the rest of his life in jail for helping her.

She had to do something. Say something.

But to whom? She was alone in her cell. Without even a guard at the door.

While the professor had also been trapped in the room with them, along with several innocent bystanders, she didn't even know whether the police had taken him into custody. Not knowing caused bile to rise up in her throat, leaving a bitter taste in her mouth.

She had no notion of Scottish law, had no idea if she had any rights or could demand a lawyer. She'd been told someone from the American consulate would be notified, but that didn't satisfy her. Upon entering the jail, she'd been locked into the cell. She hadn't been photographed. Her fingerprints hadn't

been taken. She'd answered no questions—not that any had been asked.

And she was ready to scream.

At the sound of footsteps, she peered down the hallway. A man strode toward her. She raced toward the bars. "Jason?"

"In the flesh."

He unlocked her door, his eyes glinting with familiar mischief. "I'm not accustomed to using a key."

"What happened? Why are you… How *did* you get the key? Are we making a jailbreak? What's going on?"

"First things first." The lock clicked and he opened the door, twirled her around and kissed her.

She'd never thought to have his arms around her like this again. As his lips met hers, she automatically parted her mouth, welcoming him with an uncontrollable hunger that left her trembling. She locked her hands behind his head, tugged him closer, breathing in his familiar scent and pressing her chest to his.

He released her with a grin of satisfaction.

She raised an impatient fist. "If you don't tell me right now what's happening, I'm going to deck you."

"We're being released. L.J. caught the professor's glass-smashing and crown-snatching act on tape. The professor is upstairs spilling his guts right now. And the cops found a pair of your pink panties in his room along with an old copy of your script."

"What a pervert."

He led her down the hall, up a flight of stairs to the next level where a uniformed woman handed her her personal effects. As if by mutual consent, they

waited until they were free of the police building before talking further.

The last rays of sunlight had never felt so good on her skin. She breathed in the fresh air, appreciating her freedom. "Did the professor say why he tried to frame me?"

"Jealousy. Apparently it's your fault he didn't win an Academy Award."

"What?"

"When the professor submitted his own screenplays to Simitar Studios, Quinn's first reader who actually knew the professor passed them on to you. Probably because he feared Jamison, who was head of the department, would fire him if he didn't. But then you rejected every one of his screenplays and he held a grudge."

"Did Trixie know?"

"She had nothing to do with this."

"I don't recall reading anything by a Professor Jamison."

"He used a pseudonym. And he not only blamed you for his lack of success, he fixated on you. He was sure you had turned down his brilliant screenplay so that you could sell your own story to Quinn instead."

She shook her head. "That's absurd. If Quinn wanted to buy five screenplays he could do so. The man must be delusional."

"But he's smart—to a point. After he sprayed the camera lens black, he thought no one would see him breaking the glass case. Since he picked a time when the security guard was distracted, he almost got away with it. If L.J. hadn't been backing us up, we might not be free right now."

''The professor went to all this trouble just for revenge?''

''He's unbalanced. He resents women writers. Young women writers in particular, claiming you have an advantage because…''

''Because what?''

''Because you can screw your way to the top.''

''That's ridiculous. Women in this industry are a minority. Besides, the business depends on who you know as much as on talent. I just lucked out that Quinn married one of my best friends, but he won't make an offer unless my writing knocks his socks off. What I don't understand is how did the professor know that I was coming on this trip?''

''He hired a P.I. to steal your script and follow you.''

''That's creepy. Cate and Maggie are never going to believe this.''

''Oh, yes they will.''

''What does that mean?''

He guided her straight into a restaurant. The smells of garlic and cheese, cooked ham and fresh bread assaulted her senses. She realized she was starved. ''The entire story will make news round the world.''

''Why?''

''Reporters got wind of the story. The *Book of Celts* was returned to Cornwall's library, causing more headline news. By the time I learned of the leak, there was nothing I could do. I'm sorry.''

''It's not your fault. Let's hope Quinn believes that there's no such thing as bad publicity.''

''Is that possible?''

''Quinn's unpredictable. I won't know until I go

home.'' She paused while they gave their orders to a waitress behind the bar, then took seats in a corner where the cigarette smoke wouldn't reach. ''Now, tell me why the police released you.''

He shrugged. ''They didn't look at me too carefully after L.J. showed up with the videotape. That man has credentials almost as impressive as Logan Kincaid's. Last year he almost single-handedly stopped a war between India and Pakistan from breaking out.''

She had the feeling he wasn't telling her the entire story. ''So that's it? The police never hooked into any intelligence agency to discover what you do for a living?''

''I'm here, aren't I?''

''I can barely take this all in. Everything happened so quickly. Have I thanked you yet for everything you've done?''

''You can thank me when we get to London.''

''London?''

''Yes, darling. We still have one last love scene to recreate on the London Eye.''

THE LONDON EYE, or the Millennium Wheel, at 443 feet high was the world's largest observational wheel, with pods of ellipsoid glass to give uninterrupted views over London. It took a half hour for each large car to complete one rotation, and Jason had reserved it for them alone at midnight. She didn't want to think about how he'd arranged such a feat.

Instead she took in the magnificent view. Windsor's lights to the west and Westminster's over the Thames sparkled. She picked out the Tate Gallery, the Millennium Bridge below and Covent Gardens in

the distance, but she wasn't that interested in more sightseeing, not with her early flight back to Los Angeles tomorrow. Not when this was the last time she and Jason would make love, not when her heart ached.

Quinn had suggested one fantastic setting—but when she eventually wrote this scene, she would write it with mixed emotions. Before meeting Jason, she'd never known that she could be both incredibly happy and sad at the same time. She'd finally fallen in love and was about to lose Jason. He would live the life he'd chosen, and she would return to her work and career. Alone.

Someday, this would be a romantic memory to take out and warm herself with on a rainy day. But right now, she couldn't wait to whip off her clothes, spread out the thick blanket and welcome Jason into her arms.

In the darkness, he seemed as eager as she to come together, tossing his clothes to the blanket with abandon then backing her against the glass. He swept back her hair, cupped his hands on either side of her jaw, his fingers fierce against her scalp.

"You're special to me," he told her.

Her heart thumped harder in her chest. "You're special to me, too."

"You know what I like best about you, Kimberly?"

"What?"

"Your passion for life." His fingers tangled deeper in her hair. "On the outside, you pretend to be safe, reasonable, pragmatic. But on the inside, you're bub-

bling over with a zest for life. We're alike, you and I.''

''We are?''

His hand smoothed from her jaw to her ear to the back of her neck. Hot need licked her. He tugged her closer until his lips lingered inches from hers.

''You liked the excitement of the past week, admit it.''

''I didn't like the part where the police arrested me. Or the part in jail.''

''I'm talking about eating new foods, seeing new places, making love. You loved every minute.''

Okay, she'd had a wonderful time with him. She'd fallen in love, but she bit back that particular admission. Instead she stuck out her bottom lip in a pout. ''Are you going to kiss me or what?''

''Or what.'' He chuckled and knelt between her thighs.

He'd skipped the kissing, the caressing, but when his mouth closed over her, when his fingers slipped into her heat, when his tongue found her clit, she grasped his shoulders and hung on, wished she could hold on forever.

With her emotions swinging wildly, she was more than ready to just feel. She held back nothing, letting every sensation flow through her, welcoming the budding tension, welcoming the way her breasts instantly tightened, welcoming his expertise that shot her into a warm and wonderful orgasm.

As she regained control of her ragged breathing, he stood and held her against his chest, cradling her as the last tremors dissolved. She wrapped her arms

around him, tipped back her head and whispered, "If that's your idea of foreplay, I like it."

"Good, because I plan to do it again."

AND HE HAD done it again and again. The memory comforted her all the way back to Los Angeles. Maggie met her at the airport and Kimberly turned in her script with notes to Quinn, then went home to sleep off her jet lag. Instead of blissful rest, she dreamed of Jason making love to her behind a tri-fold screen, on a boat anchored in the River Liffey, in the bathtub and on the London Eye.

He hadn't given her an address or phone number to contact him and she'd been too proud to ask. Clearly, it was over.

A week later, her pain hadn't eased at the loss of him. She missed his smile. She missed his teasing and lovemaking. Most of all, she missed staring into his blue eyes and just talking. Being practical Kimberly once again, she followed her normal routine, working eighteen-hour days, waiting for the summons to Quinn's office to hear what he thought about her research and the changes she'd made to the script.

Although she tried not to think about Jason, he constantly invaded her thoughts. Several days later, Quinn called her into his office. Looking tanned and fit from his South Pacific honeymoon, he sat behind his desk, eyeing her with speculation.

"My wife tells me you've been remarkably close-mouthed about your research."

She gestured to her script on his desk. "So what do you think?"

"I think that the love scenes in Ireland and Wales are brilliant."

At Quinn's words of praise, Kimberly's hopes soared, yet remained tinged with melancholy. Without Jason she couldn't have written those scenes. Without Jason, she couldn't have stretched the story's emotional depth.

It took a moment to recall that Quinn was waiting for her to say something. "You really like it?"

"I liked it before. Now, I love it. I adore it. It's magical, suspenseful and erotic—a can't-miss hit."

"What about the bad publicity? That crazy professor, my going to jail—"

"—created an industry buzz. A-list stars are calling me for a part and they haven't even read the script." Quinn pushed a contract offer in her direction. "You might want to have an agent look at this before you sign."

She glimpsed the six-figure advance and if she hadn't been sitting, she might have jumped up and down with joy. She'd sold her script, her baby that she'd sweated over, pampered and groomed for almost a year. Now *A Burning Obsession* was going to be made into a movie with major stars.

The news was magnificent and she wanted to celebrate, with Jason. But she couldn't call him—better to make a clean break.

In the parking garage, she picked up her cell phone, determined to celebrate with her friends. She called Cate, but she didn't answer. Neither did Maggie. Disappointed, Kimberly hung up her phone.

When a shadow loomed over her car, she reached to lock the door. Too late.

But then Jason opened the door and slid into the passenger seat as if she'd been expecting him.

"You scared the...what are you doing here?"

"And hello to you, too." He leaned over and kissed her. Her mouth, still open in surprise, welcomed him with an easy familiarity that reminded her of how much she'd missed him.

With her thoughts bubbling with excitement and passion, she broke the kiss, her curiosity at an all-time high. "Now I know I'm not dreaming but I didn't expect...didn't think...how did you...?"

He chuckled at her bewilderment. "Did you think I'd just let go of the most precious gemstone I've ever held?"

She rolled her eyes. "What did you steal now?"

"I was talking about you."

"Huh?"

"You're precious to me."

"And?" she prodded.

"I'm keeping you."

Kimberly refused to let passion overcome her good sense. "You can't keep me with you."

His eyes twinkled. "True. I have my work, but I can base my center of operations in Los Angeles. We could spend a lot of time together."

She'd missed him terribly. She loved him still. But she didn't think she could form a permanent relationship with a jewel thief. And yet, how could she send him away?

Her heart had lifted just at his presence. She couldn't take her gaze off him. He looked good in those tight jeans, a white sweater and a navy sports coat. But best of all, she liked the way she felt when

she was around him—as if she could accomplish anything. Even selling a script—thanks to him and the passion he'd inspired.

"Quinn loved the script." Jason chuckled.

"He said the love scenes were brilliant."

"Mmm."

"You stole my heart."

For the first time his eyes lost some of their amusement. "Say that again."

"You heard me. I love you."

"And you waited until now to tell me because—"

"I wasn't going to tell you at all. Forget I said that."

"Why weren't you going to tell me?"

"Because we have no future."

"I love you, too, I won't give you up and I've decided to make L.A. my home."

"But—"

"That was before I took a job with the Shey Group."

Her heart stuttered. "You did?"

"That's right. You are now looking at the Shey Group's number-one thief."

"I don't understand."

"I'll still be stealing, but this time I'll be on your side of the law."

"What about your record?"

He snapped his fingers. "Erased."

"The warrants for your arrest?"

"Gone. Ka-poof."

"How?"

"Logan Kincaid pulled some favors in exchange for my help over the next two years. You're looking

at a solid citizen. My new name is Jason Connors. So what do you think?''

Overwhelmed, she didn't know what to say. ''Did you do this for me?''

''For us.''

''Well, in that case it's time to begin researching my next script.'' She leaned over to him for another kiss. ''What do you think of a movie that begins with two lovers in the front seat of a car?''

''Sounds perfect. Right down to the protagonist removing her blouse.''

She fumbled for the buttons. Buttons he'd already undone. He'd surprised her again and she hoped he kept doing so for a long, long time.

* * * * *

Look for more HEROES, INC. *titles
from Susan Kearney next month in*
Essence of Midnight,
*a Harlequin Special Release anthology,
and in November and December
from Harlequin Intrigue.*

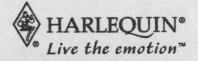

HARLEQUIN®
Temptation.

When the spirits are willing...
Anything can happen!

Welcome to the Inn at Maiden Falls, Colorado. Once a brothel in the 1800s, the inn is now a successful honeymoon resort. Only, little does anybody guess that all that marital bliss comes with a little supernatural persuasion....

Don't miss this fantastic new miniseries. Watch for:

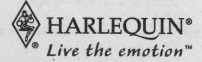

HARLEQUIN®

Temptation.

New York Times bestselling author

VICKI LEWIS THOMPSON

**celebrates Temptation's 20th anniversary—
and her own—in:**

#980

OLD ENOUGH TO KNOW BETTER

When twenty-year-old PR exec Kasey Braddock accepts
her co-workers' dare to hit on the gorgeous new landscaper,
she's excited. Finally, here's her chance to prove to her
friends—and herself—that she's woman enough to entice
a man and leave him drooling. After all, she's old enough
to know what she wants—and she wants Sam Ashton.
Luckily, he's not complaining....

Available in June wherever Harlequin books are sold.

If you enjoyed what you just read,
then we've got an offer you can't resist!

Take 2 bestselling love stories FREE!

Plus get a FREE surprise gift!

HARLEQUIN® *Blaze*™
HARLEQUIN® *Temptation*®

Single in South Beach

Nightlife on the Strip just got a little hotter!

Join author Joanne Rock as she takes you back to Miami Beach and its hottest singles' playground. Club Paradise has staked its claim in the decadent South Beach nightlife and the women in charge are determined to keep the sexy resort on top. So what will they do with the hot men who show up at the club?

GIRL GONE WILD
Harlequin Blaze #135
May 2004

DATE WITH A DIVA
Harlequin Blaze #139
June 2004

HER FINAL FLING
Harlequin Temptation #983
July 2004

Don't miss the continuation of this red-hot series from Joanne Rock!

Look for these books at your favorite retail outlet.

www.eHarlequin.com

HBSSB2

HARLEQUIN®
Live the emotion™

www.eHarlequin.com

BLAZE™

ISBN 0-373-79142-9

AVAILABLE NOW:

#137 INDECENT
Sleeping with Secrets
Tori Carrington

#138 A BURNING OBSESSION
Heroes, Inc.
Susan Kearney

#139 DATE WITH A DIVA
Single in South Beach
Joanne Rock

#140 THE SEX DIET
Rhonda Nelson

HARLEQUIN®

138
June

Blaze

HEROES INC.

USA *TODAY* Bestselling Author

A BURNING OBSESSION

Susan Kearney

Obsession can never be too dark or too deep

$4.50 U.S. $5.25 CAN.